PRAISE FOR
A PLACE FOR SNAKES TO BREED

"Finn writes with the precision and eloquence of Cormac McCarthy, an understanding of what Jack London called 'the submerged tenth,' and the brutality of Nelson Algren and David Goodis. *A Place for Snakes to Breed* is a novel that will be studied by students and scholars, and serve as a model of how a book should be written for writers." —Eric Miles Williamson, author of *East Bay Grease* and *Welcome to Oakland*.

"Finn's sinewy sentences whose movements you will not predict (and which you will read several times to savor and to try to piece out how he got there) turns *A Place for Snakes to Breed* into much more than a story about a troubled youth on a journey through the underworld. This is the world of a gifted writer who knows that the impoverished, the defective, and the hopeless is as complex as that of the upper-class characters that populate so much best-selling drivel." —Ron Cooper, author of *Purple Jesus* and *All My Sins Remembered*

A PLACE FOR
SNAKES TO BREED

BOOKS BY PATRICK MICHAEL FINN

From the Darkness Right Under Our Feet
A Martyr for Suzy Kosasovich
A Place for Snakes to Breed

PATRICK MICHAEL FINN

A PLACE FOR
SNAKES TO BREED

DOWN&OUT
BOOKS

Down & Out Books
3959 Van Dyke Road, Suite 265
Lutz, FL 33558
DownAndOutBooks.com

Cover design by Shmael Graphics

ISBN: 1-64396-207-8
ISBN-13: 978-1-64396-207-8

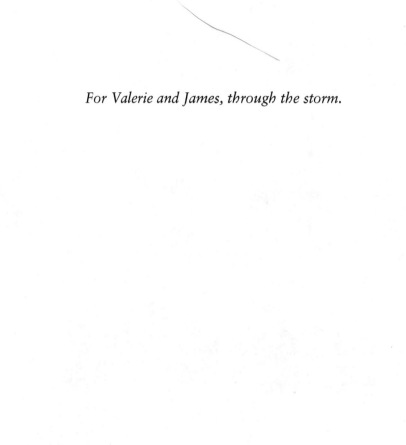

For Valerie and James, through the storm.

"The lemon groves are sunken, down a three- or four-foot retaining wall, so that one looks directly into their dense foliage, too lush, unsettlingly glossy, the greenery of nightmare; the fallen eucalyptus bark is too dusty, a place for snakes to breed."
—Joan Didion, "Some Dreamers of the Golden Dream"

1

By now she knew her father slept hardest in the hour before sunrise and that by the depth of his snoring she could move through the house to pack up her shit without worrying about waking him to face the hairy scene he'd make about trying to get her to stay.

She crossed into his room and took his wallet from the dresser, behind his snoring and down out the window in the wasted riverbed the coyotes yelping and bawling for food in the dark and remembering the sound of his voice, tired but gentle, she winced as she pulled five twenties out. If there had been more she would have taken it. She knew she'd need more, much more, and soon. Two days soon. A worry that lasted as long as a breath.

Darkness crawled into every window and covered her feet like sludge. And then the dim green light in the kitchen from the clock on the stove, a signal at the bottom of a black water lake. She looked in some drawers for the phone book and the freezer kicked on and she went stiff and the Percocet drained from her face and the needles of pain in her split lips and swollen eyes and the stitches in her brow pulsed in waves so radiant it was like the Mexican girls were beating her up all over again. She wavered and braced herself against the sink when she felt her stomach gurgle and brought her fist to her mouth until the sickness passed and then padded to her room for two more pills she swallowed without water.

She found the phone book and sat cross-legged on the plastic floor and read by the flame of her cigarette lighter: Blood Banks, Garbage Collection, Lumber, Optical, Oil Change, Ready Mixed Concrete, Tire Dealers, Tool Repair. Then back a few pages to Taxi Companies When she stood again the dial tone sounded like a woman humming a love gospel, a woman in a barn or an empty church. She almost sang along and a point of light in the center of her head shone through her voice, her whisper like passionate orgasm and the taxi lady on the other end said, "I'm sorry?"

"For what?" she breathed back. "Wait, wait," she said. "I mean four twenty-six Cajalco Road. Cajalco Road in Hufford."

"No, sweetie, I got that already. I need to know where you're headed."

"Where I'm headed?"

"Where do you want the cab to take you when the driver arrives?"

"When's he coming? When's he going to get here?"

Now she was nervous that speaking through split lips made her sound stupid. When she blinked fast the swell in her eyes tightened and stung. She couldn't stop herself from touching the stitches, still tender and a little damp. And it wasn't until the taxi lady said, "You still there, dear?" that she remembered she was even on the phone at all.

"Is he here yet?" she whispered. "Is he here yet, the taxi?"

"Hufford's way out. Probably take him twenty, maybe thirty more minutes."

Then she thought about staying, putting the money back into his wallet instead of sneaking off like an ingrate shit snake skanky little barn garbage Okie.

"Honey, I've got to know where you want the driver to take you when he gets there. Where it is you're headed. The driver needs to know that when he picks you up."

"The beach."

"The beach? You know how much a cab ride is from Hufford all the way out to the beach? That's about eighty miles. Good lord, sweetie, do you really know where you're going?"

The last dose had disappeared entirely and every cell in her face turned into a shard of glass and sliced. Her father coughed and tossed. He cleared his throat.

"Anywhere," she said. "I got a hundred bucks, honest to God. A hundred bucks. Wherever that will get me. Just send him. I'll show him the money as soon as he gets here. Please. Just send him. Please. Just send him. I'll go wherever he can take me. But I don't have much time. I have to go now. Now. You know what I mean?"

After a week he finally admitted that his missing dog King was dead. He sat in his truck out front of his house, sweating through the hazy sun hot through the windshield, the motor off and the windows up. A brushfire had started over in Wild Horse Canyon earlier that day and the whole truck shook against the violence of the winds storming down from the high desert and down through the Cajon Pass and battering the glass with splintered twigs and grit. Distant hillsides burned with rivers of flames that blew tumbleweeds into feedlots and stables and barns like wheels of wrath sent down from a mountain of punishing judgement.

For the last six nights he had called for King over the back fence and had beamed a Maglite below only to find a vicious snarl of mesquite and scrub oak and buckbrush growing in aimless arrangement along a stretch of dried-out riverbed dense with a flora of spines. One night he stood calling for three hours straight, his voice finally falling to a rasping reverberation that returned an extra man crawling aged up the bluff until neither his strained gullet nor ringing ears could tell the difference between what was hollered and what was heard, King, King, King, King, King, an aftersound that played in his brain a lunatic preoccupation long after he left the fence and lay awake slack with defeat. He lived alone and had no neighbors to disturb. Next to his house was a wasted space of overgrown mustard brush that spread to another squat house that looked a lot like his. Bare white stucco with a door and a few little windows and beyond that some property a few acres away with a fifth-wheeler and two rusted sheds. Then down the road where it ended at a rise of malformed boulders a house that some nights hosted a ragged traffic of slurring beer drunk laughter in the driveway where black shapes of men swayed and drank in the yellow light that glowed from the garage.

There was still an hour before sunset. He loaded up two blankets and a carton of black plastic bags into the flatbed and drove to a spot east of the interstate and parked behind a stand of smoke trees and carried the blankets to a rocky switchback that angled down into the riverbed. When he got to the bottom he wavered in the hot gusts. He stood for a while under the shade of a cottonwood and wiped his forehead. Sand blew up into his eyes and when he closed his mouth, he tasted smoke and dirt and ash.

The walk west was even hotter against the hovering sun through sand and clusters of dead scrub. He trudged as though through a low flood and eyed the larger spaces of shade where King would have been dragged by the coyotes or pack dogs that had killed him. He crouched to rest then walked back into the bare torch of sunlight and the dirty wind of ash and sand and smoke. Another hour passed before he noticed he was no longer sweating. Just burning.

When he finally found King, he only recognized him by the shape of his body.

The animal lay in a patch of charred sand, hairless with blackened flesh that glistened as though greased. His snout and both pairs of legs had been bound with wires. Weldon moved though the blowing smoke and dust, squinting, and urged himself to stand over King's remains. He had his work gloves in his

4

back pocket and he struggled in his trembling to pull them on. The sunset was stained with a haze of motionless brown gas and strings of skinny crows squalled in gradual escalation and vanished into the dimming sky.

He crouched and took King by his front legs and turned him over and saw that his head had been crushed in at his ear. He stood up and yelled, "Hey!" He pivoted in every direction, stomping, and yelled, "Hey!" But he was yelling at nothing but hot, vacant nature.

He wrapped King's front end into one of the garbage bags and his back end into the other and carried him to the blankets and rolled and tucked them over the bags on all sides and hoisted him over his shoulder. The stink of gasoline and bad meat stung right through the bags and blankets. He winced at the odor as he dragged himself through the sand.

By the time he reached the top of the switchback, he was gasping. He put the bundle of blankets on the seat beside him and kept one hand on it the whole way home and once he got there hung a mechanic's lamp from the fence and got a shovel from the garage and forced the edge into the soil with the weight of his boot and hoisted out clumps and tossed them aside, the bundle of blankets lit with the chipped and rusted vigil hanging from the fence.

It was nine when he finished filling the hole and after he did, he carried the shovel for a few steps then dragged it across the yard and slouched back into the house with his arms hanging. His telephone was ringing.

A girl's voice on the other end. "This Weldon Holt?"

"Yeah. Who's this?"

"Your daughter. Your daughter Tammy."

He gunned his truck to the San Bernardino Greyhound station, which had the only Western Union window open at that hour. Tammy had called him from a bus station payphone in El Paso,

Texas. She needed to get to California and asked if she could stay with him for a while. He asked her what kind of trouble she was in and she said she had to hang up. A whole line of people waiting the use the phone.

He wired her the money and when she got it, she called him back on the pay phone just like he'd told her to.

"What time does your bus come in?"

"Tomorrow some time. Maybe twenty-four hours they said."

"What time is it in El Paso?"

"I don't know. I don't have a watch."

"Look for a clock on one of the walls."

"It's eleven."

"Ten here in California. Now I want you to tell me what's going on."

"I can't talk long."

"How long do you have?"

"Five minutes. Three."

"Five or three?"

"Five."

"All right. Then tell me."

"Mom strangled me with a radio cord."

"What the hell do you mean?"

"She strangled me with the electric cord on the radio."

Weldon squinted and squeezed the back of his neck. "You call the police?"

"No, no. I was listening to the rock station in my room. I wasn't supposed to be listening to the radio anyhow."

Weldon switched the phone from one side of his face to the other. A bus pulled out of the terminal and headlights like two moons crossed the window.

"It's because of church," she said. "I'm only supposed to listen to the radio when Mom's around, and only to the gospel station."

"When did all this happen, Tammy?"

"Two days ago. She's crazy. She found all my makeup and took it out to the driveway and broke it all. Just stomped on it.

I have to go."

"Are you all right?"

"Yeah. I have to go."

"Call me as soon as you get in. Doesn't matter what time. Middle of the night, I don't care."

He watched the fires in the hills that night from his kitchen window drinking coffee at the sink. The flames twisted like banners that roared into orbs of yellow light. Out back underneath a patch of brown earth lay King. How many days had it been since he'd taken his last breath? Maybe he didn't feel anything. Maybe they'd crushed the side of his head in first. He knew it had taken more than one to murder him.

He saw her sitting on the other side of the terminal in washed jeans and black sneakers. She was tucked into the end of a bench against a purple school backpack with her arms crossed, her face held by a lightless dejection that was much deeper than the exhaustion of the trip. She looked a bit younger than seventeen. He'd expected to greet her as soon as he got there, but instead he sat on the nearest bench to hide under his lowered cap.

He stood and gestured with a half wave. She had light brown hair and she was almost chubby. When she looked up there was no relief, not even a thin smile. She grabbed her backpack and slung it over her shoulder and said Hi he same way someone would say Bye before boarding another bus to head back home.

"Hello, Tammy."

In the front seat of the truck, she watched San Bernardino crawl by in the night. Chain-link fences and barbwire that ran alongside the Santa Fe switchyards. Yellow streetlights and billboards for Mexican beer.

"Some California," she said. "Goddamn dump."

She looked at him once and asked him if he lived here.

"No, I'm out in Hufford. It's not like this. It's out in the country."

"The country. Is the rest of California this shitty?"

"I imagine you're pretty wiped out after that trip."

"I'm pretty glad to get the hell out of that house is what I am."

They were out of the city and on the dark roads that passed a few ranches and feedlots.

"Stinks out here," she said. "Does it stink this bad where you live?"

"Sometimes. Not usually."

"Looks the same as Oklahoma. Smells the same too. Might as well just stayed there."

"You all right, Tammy?"

"All right from what?"

"From your mother hurting you like that."

"I'll be all right as long as I'm away from that crazy bitch. I don't even have makeup. She took it all and smashed it all up in the driveway."

"We can get you makeup tomorrow. And we'll get you some clothes if you want. You need a bed too. I'll take the couch and you can have my bed."

"I'd rather have the couch. I don't like sleeping in other people's beds."

She wouldn't look at him when she spoke. She was watching the ditches and fence lines they passed, her arms crossed.

"You know I tried to send you money, Tammy. For years. But your mother kept sending it back."

"She told me. Said your money was the devil's money and didn't want it in the house."

They'd pulled onto Interstate 15 and now it crossed the riverbed. He imagined a crew of maniacs with torches and wires and gasoline closing in on every lost dog in the world.

Outcall only. No driver. No BS.

It was a little after ten when they called, slurring, to give her their address somewhere in northeast Mesa. They sounded young, like they'd been drinking since about four, high school young, and now six hours of booze had flooded to their hairless red boners. "How much is it going to cost?" And behind the voice covered laughter and some country music on the radio.

"We can talk about that when I get there."

The driver was silent the whole drive. When she asked him if she could smoke he just shrugged. Under the moon an outline of jagged hills as they neared the destination. "I'll be a half hour," she said. "Wait and I'll give you an extra ten. Will you wait?"

The driver nodded and told her he would.

When she knocked they shut off the music and their riot inside quieted and they gathered around the door to see her and the light from inside the house poured past them and spilled onto the stoop by her shoes. She was the oldest person in the house.

She glanced into the next room and found a boy facedown on the couch, a waterfall of vomit down the cushions to the carpet. Then the radio kicked on, keep it country, and the boys hooted and shoved each other and chugged from beer cans they popped open with discharges they sprayed at each other. They shot glances at her and she realized she hadn't had a dream in months. Or couldn't remember any.

A chubby boy with a face hardened by nerves elbowed his way through the others and blurted, "Can we fuck? I mean, can I fuck you?"

Behind him tittering moon-faced boys swilling Natural Light. She sneered. "No, you sure as shit can't," she said.

His face was about to fold into a sharp, furious sob, his eyes widening and his mouth bent at the corners. And then his eyes flashed as though he'd just gotten wonderful news. "Will you suck my dick?"

"Hell, go on and suck your own dick."

The host, the boy who had opened the door, was wearing a Mopar cap with a pinched bill. He appeared in the kitchen and asked her if he could talk to her alone for a minute. He led her down a hallway past his parents' bedroom and then into his own, and the first thing she noticed was the dry aquarium on his dresser. It shone a beautiful sinister blue in the darkness. When he closed the door, she told him to keep it open.

"That's my snake," he said.

He was a well-built boy who looked like he played football and ate lots of steak. "It's a real rattlesnake," he said.

When she peered into the glass, she saw that it was indeed a rattler and she wondered what her deathbed regrets might be. The snake was gray-brown and coiled and she could see its white rattle at rest in the gravel at the bottom of the tank.

"I thought it was against the law to keep a rattlesnake."

"Yeah, but I'm keeping it anyway."

"How'd you get it?"

"I caught it in a box over at the Tonto National Forest!"

He lowered his head and wiped at his nose with the back of his hand. "Now listen," he said. "Don't get mad," he said.

Glass shattered in the kitchen and the boys laughed. Shit oh shit oh shit she heard one of them yell.

"You going to get mad?" he asked.

"Well how the hell can I answer that if I don't know what you're going to tell me?"

"All right, look. I don't know who called you. I didn't call you. I swear. And I'm sorry you came all the way out here, but none of us have any money."

She shoved him out of the way and marched through the house then out the door to an entirely vacant street. She looked up and down. No taxi. She thrashed and cursed and flung her purse to the pavement and put her arms over her head and hissed No a few times before she slouched over to the curb and sat and let her head fall into her hands. When she looked back over her shoulder, she saw fifteen black bodies at the window.

She banged on the door like an angry neighbor stomping over to complain about the noise. The country music on the radio fell dead in a vanish of twang and lonesome sorrow. Some boys opened the door but the host boy was not among them. They watched her, blinking with their wet boy mouths open and swaying.

"I'm not sucking your dicks neither," she said.

She strolled past them with a gait of pure superiority. "I'm only here to use the phone," she said. "Where's the phone book?"

Two boys pulled drawer after drawer until one of them found it and she snatched it from him and tore through the pages until she found the taxis. As it was past midnight, she had to call five different taxis before she found one that was willing to pick her up. She said, "Suck it!" to each dispatcher who told her no. The boys were scared. They watched the floor and held their empty cans.

The taxi would be another hour, so she stood at the living room window and waited. Someone switched the radio on and she snapped her head and said, "Turn that hayseed horseshit off."

One by one the boys fell away to the end of their night. The hour passed and still no taxi and her head rushed with rage and a storm of curses. Her legs ached from standing at the window. She glanced at the boys passed out on the floor. She heard someone getting sick in the bathroom.

With the first light of dawn, she knew no taxi would come and headed down the hallway to the host boy's room so she could wake him to see if there was a car in the garage and if he was old enough to drive it. The bedroom door was closed and when she knocked twice, he didn't answer.

She wondered how long she'd stood there waiting for him to answer because when she opened the door the room was filled with sunlight that shone through the window and over the boy's dead body, blue and sprawled on the carpet, the rattlesnake coiled in the corner and watching his captor dispassionately. The boy's eyes stared at the ceiling from his blue face.

When the shock of the room finally seized her, she whispered the first prayer she'd made in fifteen years. The snake heard her. He raised his head and shook his rattle. She fled through the rooms of sleeping boys and out to the vacant morning and she ran down the middle of the empty street and the boy's blue face and the death rattling snake chased her.

Slow down, baby Tammy.

Here's your bib and your crib and your pipe and your noose.

We'll bite you on that chubby little ass and suck you out until you're blue too.

At Walmart they looked at a catalog for her new bed and she pointed at the first one she saw.

"Now that's a child's bed," he told her. "It'll be too small for you. Take your time. Pick out a nice one."

She turned a couple pages and pointed at a double and said, "There. That one's fine."

"You sure? You hardly looked."

"Yeah, it's fine."

"It'll take a couple days for them to deliver it. Offer's still good for my bed if you want it."

"That's all right. Hey, can I get some clothes?"

She sped through the racks and didn't like that he was standing there. When she looked at him, he decided to wander off.

"Hey," she called. "I'm going to try these on."

He waited near the fitting rooms where the attendant, a heavy woman with a hanging goiter, eyed him distrustfully. "My daughter," he said and she nodded, though her expression didn't change.

When she came out, she had a big bundle of clothes in her arms.

"Let me help you," he said.

"That's all right."

She grabbed a shopping cart and laid the bundle over it and pushed it to the makeup aisle and grabbed from the display pencils and tubes of lipstick and mascara and bottles of nail polish and thick-handled brushes and stuck them all in the cart.

"I guess that's all," she said.

She got some candy bars and gum and mints at the checkout and once everything was paid for and bagged and they were heading for the exit, she stopped and said, "Shit, I forgot. You mind getting me a carton of Marlboro reds? I'll be out front."

He felt like no-account trash buying her cigarettes, especially a whole carton. He bought them anyway and pretended to forget they were father and daughter.

The Victory Tabernacle was no bigger than a garage and the inside felt even smaller, especially with how many yowling followers were packed inside waving their arms in the air and jabbering all sorts of nonsense. Other than the homemade-looking cross at the front of the room you wouldn't have known it was a church at all. They somehow got a set of drums in the corner and a man playing a guitar and a preacher yelling "Praise Him! Praise Him!" before launching into a whole storm of blabber himself that sounded like a baby playing with a box of puppies.

Darna drove right past the hand-painted sign just off the road outside of Cottonwood Canyon. Grandpa Lady yelled, "Stop, stop, stop!" and the tires skidded and the baby started screaming and Tammy's ears went white with burning shrieks.

"We're late!" Darna snapped. She sucked her cigarette down to the brown filter and pitched it out the window and it spun into the backseat and battered both Tammy and the baby with cherry sparks and this time when the baby wailed it blinded her with an attack of panic and rage and regret and then love.

"What in the fuck?" Darna said. She strained to see the backseat in the rearview and then she strained to turn her head, back and forth and back and forth like a sex store laugh gadget. They'd gone down the road a good mile beyond the church as though they'd all forgotten where they were supposed to be in the first place. She sped, braked, sped again, and finally made a U-turn.

They'd been up for five days on a fresh batch of peanut butter biker crank, the last of which they torched up in a pipe in the bathroom once Grandpa Lady took the baby inside. They had on some of Grandpa Lady's heavy, ankle-length dresses and they waved the smoke out of the stall and with the white fire in their throats, they found themselves devoured by the gospel guitar and gospel drums and gospel tongues chewing straight through the wall.

"You've got to love Jesus Christ," Darna said. "Do you know Him in your heart?"

"I do," Tammy said. Her eyes welled and reddened.

"Let Him into your heart, girl."

"I'll let him."

Darna took her by the arm and ran her into the church through all the damp bodies holding themselves in mid-spin and every horn in Tammy's head played along with the music of praise and called back to the preacher in a glowing thrum that cleared the fog out of her eyes and the preacher lowered her to her knees and the drummer smashed the cymbals so the church filled with a series of bell bursts and the congregants laid their hands over her head and at first she was afraid they were pushing her straight down to Hell and she lowered her face and wept out all the liquid of sin running from her brains and the preacher stood above her with his hands raised and told her she was saved by the Blood of the Lamb.

They leaped and sang while they held themselves weeping. A rapture had pierced their pounding hearts with lances of fire and the blood in their veins turned from evil boiling rivers to brooks.

Darna embraced her with her bony limbs and barked into her ear over the music and Holy Ghost Power, "We can't get fucked up anymore. And we've got to quit dancing and sucking dick."

"I know it."

"You say you do, and I say I do, but it's easy to slip."

"I won't slip."

"Help me, Tammy. You're saved by the Blood of the Lamb

and I need your power to help me stay straight."

"I'll help you. I won't slip."

"You can't slip. If you do, if we both do, I'm cutting both of our throats."

"All right."

"I mean it. I'll kill us both. Because when you turn your back on Jesus, there's only once place to go and that's death."

She became the blanket and the couch and sat without mood, pacified by the television. She slept there every night even after he'd assembled her bed in the extra room. He wondered if she might be afraid of the dark and that's why she kept the television running at all hours. The only time she got up was when she took her soda and went out back to smoke. He wasn't sure when it was she fixed herself anything to eat.

She came in sour one afternoon. "I didn't want to say nothing, since you're letting me stay here and all, but it smells like cow shit hell out there."

"It'll get better when it cools off. The feedlots have whole ponds of it."

"Can't I just smoke inside?"

"I'm sorry, no."

"Why not?"

"Because smoke smells bad."

"Smells better than whatever the hell's out there."

"I rent this house and it's all the house I can afford on my disability. And the lease says no smoking. Cigarette smoke sticks to the walls, the ceiling. If the landlord tried to sell the place, I'd get charged a load of money for him to repaint everything."

"You don't have to explain everything to me like a damn explain machine. I'm not some dumb hick."

"Look, if you already had the answers to your questions, I wouldn't have to explain a damn thing."

A grand production of rolling her eyes and shaking her head.

Then she scowled and stuck a cigarette in her mouth and lit it up right there in the kitchen.

"What the hell did I just tell you, Tammy?"

She shrugged and raised her eyebrows. "I heard you."

"What point are you trying to make? What is it you want to prove?"

"I got rights," she said. "I got rights and I got problems. Problems you don't understand."

She blew one last white puff at the ceiling then opened the door and flicked it into the yard and with her head lowered grabbed the blanket off the couch and went to her room and pulled her door shut.

He bought her a television the next day, a radio, a dresser from Goodwill for all the clothes she hadn't touched since they'd bought them weeks before. He even got her a few plastic ashtrays and told her she could smoke in her room as long as she cracked the window.

She stood in the doorway and watched him set everything up. She thanked him, but her mood didn't get any better.

"You can watch whatever you want here," he said. He was adjusting the antenna for a clearer picture. "And you can listen to whatever you damn well please on this here radio. You know that, right?"

"You trying to make up for yesterday buying me that?"

"I just thought you'd like your own space."

"And now you're letting me smoke in the house."

"Just in here."

"Just in here. Whatever. Look, I'm thankful, but it wouldn't mean as much to me than if you just told me you were sorry."

"I am sorry."

"Sorry doesn't mean anything if you don't know what you're sorry for."

He glanced at the television. The picture was fine on most of the channels. "I'm sorry I was pretty hard on you. Telling you what to do."

"And you could have asked me what was wrong when I got mad. And you could have asked me about my problems when I told you I had them."

"You're right. I understand and you're right."

She shrugged and slid the window open and set an ashtray on the sill. She lit a cigarette and sat on the edge of her bed.

"I'll leave you now," he said, and she nodded once without looking at him.

He didn't see much of her after that. The television and the radio were loud constants even so late into the night that he had to keep his door shut and stick wads of cotton in his ears.

And then one night while he was sitting in the kitchen drinking coffee in the dark, her mother called.

"Tammy there with you?"

"She sure as hell is here, and she's safe here."

"Safe?"

"Safe."

"If getting loaded together is safe then I guess you two are doing fine. I was just wondering where she'd ended up."

"Goddamn you."

"Goddamn me?"

"Strangling your own daughter."

"You two must be having a high time. Enjoy yourselves. Drink up and snort yourselves into the same grave."

"Hold it."

"What."

"I quit liquor a long time ago. Fifteen years. Tammy's in her room."

She was quiet for a while and she could tell he was sober. "She told you I tried to strangle her?"

"You and that crazy damn church."

"She's lying to you."

"What the hell kind of church you take her to?"

"You think I go to church? Think I'd go to any church after how my life ended up?"

He fell silent. He watched the hills shaped in the dark by a low bright moon. The fires had long been put out, but nobody had started rebuilding. The landscape was black at night and black during the day.

"Not that I haven't wanted to," she said.

"Wanted to what."

"Strangle her. She's lying to you through her lipstick. Girl she used to go to school with, her mother strangled her to death with the radio cord. Crazy woman in a crazy church. Crazy preacher husband too. Thirteen children. Now twelve. Woman's on death row waiting on the gas chamber."

He heard the muffled bombast of canned comedy laughter from Tammy's bedroom, like a boxcar of lunatics dropped into a canyon.

"I didn't strangle her, Weldon. She ran away."

"Why didn't you call here sooner? She's been here a whole month."

"I was glad she was finally gone. Most of me still is. I didn't even call the police when she took off. Figured they'd call me when she ended up in jail. She's already been arrested twice."

"What the hell for?"

"Shoplifting once. Then drugs. Acid and cocaine. I'm holding down three jobs here for the legal bills. Then medical bills."

"What medical bills?"

"Shit, Weldon. Tammy's a drunk. A fall on her face drunk. A drug addict. And she's already has two abortions."

He couldn't hold these lives, couldn't catch these lives he'd hurled away now that they'd fallen back into his arms. His legs buckled. He wanted to sit on the floor but was afraid he'd fall over if he tried to.

"I drove her myself. A clinic all the way in Santa Fe. She's worn all the care out of me. What care I had left, anyway. You still there?"

"Yes."

"I remarried. Divorced now. I have another daughter. Ten

years old and she doesn't want to talk to me much. Keeping three jobs I'm hardly ever around for her to talk to. Cashier at Luby's, cashier at the Kroger mart. Then I work in the cafeteria at the high school. Boys in the lunch line make jokes to each other when they see me. Half of them screwed Tammy and I guess they like to have a laugh about it. She never told me who the fathers were and I don't think she knew anyway. I guess I see them in the lunch line. She ripped all the care out of me. But sometimes I can't help worrying. Wondering if she's dead. Like tonight."

"She's fine here."

"No, she isn't."

"She's in her room. Watching television."

"I didn't think I'd like hearing your voice."

He didn't need to ask her why.

"And I was right," she said. "Goodbye."

There wasn't a lock on Tammy's door and he didn't knock before he opened it. The television was so loud she didn't hear him enter. She was standing by the window torching a sheet of foil and sucking the crank smoke through a straw. A big brown bottle of Seagram's by her feet.

He called her name. She dropped the foil and when he moved closer, she pushed him with both hands and yelled at him to get out.

Her voice became an evil thing on old fumes that clouded his face. She pushed him again, behind her the cartoonish commercial music booming, singing sponges and dancing bars of soap. Even enraged her face hung in stupor. She slapped him twice and he grabbed her wrists.

She kicked at him and pulled herself away and tottered backward. "I knew you'd get on my ass. You're just an old drunk anyway."

She snagged the bottle off the floor and took a long swallow that squeezed her whole face. "So I don't see what sort of right you have even being in here."

He reached for the bottle and they wrestled on either side of the bottle until he yanked it away and recoiled at the splash, the first bottle he'd held in fifteen years and its heft and its gas were smiles happy to see him until they turned and laughed at him, even laughing when he poured them down the toilet. He forgot about Tammy and then remembered Tammy and then forgot about her again with a deep and ignorant neglect and he dropped the bottle and it popped its brown glass all over the floor and when he knelt to pick it up the fangs on the broken neck sliced his hand open and he lost his breath and felt a cheap fever rise into his face and he held himself and rocked and bled and somehow made it to the kitchen for rags under the sink.

He knew she was gone as soon as he called her name and it echoed through the empty house.

He saw her as soon as he turned on the headlights. Fifty yards down the road with her backpack. He idled alongside her while she pretended she didn't see him and that she was set to walk all the way back to Oklahoma if it took her a year and ten pairs of shoes. She finally stopped and got in and filled the cab with an ethanol reek so thick he had to crack the window.

"Wait, stop," she said, then opened the door and stuck her head out and gagged and got sick on the dirt.

The road dead ended a few miles up and he turned around and the headlights swept across two little houses dark in yards of dirt with a truck in front of one and a rusted RV in front of the other. He passed his own house and kept driving because he was afraid if he took her home she would leave in the middle of the night. Now she was crying in her hands and shaking her head.

He drove them aimlessly and for so long that he didn't know where they were. Colton or Fontana. Machine shops and tire yards on streets he'd never seen. She'd stopped crying and had fallen asleep.

At an empty intersection stop light she startled him by speaking. "Are you going to kick me out?"

"No."

The light went green and he drove on.

"I lied to you about everything," she said, her voice breaking. "Mama never hurt me. I'm all messed up. You don't even know. I've been lying bad to you."

"I know it."

"About everything."

"Your mother called me tonight. She told me."

"What did she tell you?"

"She told me she was worried about you."

"What did she say about me?"

"She told me about your troubles."

They'd been sitting parked in front of the house. He'd cut the engine but left the headlights on and saw the twinkle of broken glass in the road.

"I can't have any booze in the house," he told her. "I see liquor all the time. Gas stations. Grocery stores. I hardly even notice it. But I almost drank down the rest of your whiskey. I didn't think I was that close anymore. But my God."

He'd forgotten about the gash in his hand until he noticed he was holding it up and that it had opened again. He lowered it so she wouldn't notice the blood running down his arm.

"You can't drink anymore. Or smoke up that shit off the foil. For you and for me."

He helped her to bed and felt the blood crust on his hand and pulse pang after pang of anguish straight from his heart. He washed the slice and tore up a shirt and wrapped it with duct tape and the pain half lifted. He sat where she'd sat. First the couch and then out in the truck opposite his own empty seat and the motionless steering wheel. He went in to check on her. She lay with her eyes open to the ceiling. Eyes that held a wreckage of the night and the rest of her life.

The outside sleep and the inside sleep.

The outside night and the inside dawn tearing through the womb with its fire.

* * *

The high school her father was driving her to was going to be a disaster by the looks of the neighborhood they passed as they neared it. Squat white stucco storefronts with Spanish stenciled on the windows over colored drawings of wedding cakes and girls in long gowns and loaves of bread and steaming burritos. A hair salon next to a liquor store with bars over the doors and then a record store with posters of mean-looking Mexican cowboys in matching black shirts and pistols and whips.

"You scared?" he asked her.

"I guess so. A little."

"It's a scary thing heading into a strange new place," he said. "Tammy, I hope you don't hate me for making you do this. For making you go to school. You understand it's the only way to make this work. To make your whole life work."

"I know it."

And she had to know it. If she didn't follow through, she wouldn't be able to live with him anymore. He'd told her so.

"And I hope you know I'm not punishing you."

"I don't think that."

Nausea hummed in her once among the jostling sprawl of a thousand students, the whole population of the town she'd come from. A low curdling murmur that sounded both tired and enraged and that matched their sullen mouths. Boys with long frosted hair like heavy metal faggots. Mexicans in black jerseys and baseball caps with pictures of swords and pirates in football helmets.

You couldn't see anything in the bathroom mirrors. Faces looked like metal stains etched with deep scratches. The Mexican girls jammed themselves around the sinks to tease and fix and spray their clouds of curly black hair. She was surprised none of them spoke Spanish.

"Ow," one of them said.

"You're pulling too hard."

"I'm not even."

"You're using too much Net."

"I'm not."

They had on skirts and dark lipstick and their eyebrows were penciled, like they were all heading out to go dancing at eight in the morning.

The bell rang and finally her turn in the stall, which reeked so bad her cheeks puffed with a hot gag. She looked up and saw a bloody pad stuck to the back of the door, swipes of brown blood for a nose and a pair of eyes staring down at her in a ridiculous grimace of filth.

Textbooks she knew she would never read and stacks of make-up work folders she knew she'd never complete. And the students were all a truckload of retarded animals so loud and senseless in their wandering up and down the rows of desks that the teachers could say nothing beyond calling for a quiet that would never fall. She couldn't understand how a teacher could come to work in such a jail every morning. She tried to imagine how the alarm clock would sound and then feel in the dark for a teacher in the bed to have to get up to face such raving beasts every day, every day, every day. The animals would leave after twelfth grade or sooner if they dropped out. But Jesus Christ the teachers had to stay until they were a few years from dead. She couldn't understand why a teacher would choose to teach here, and she decided it was because for whatever reason they hadn't been able to make a choice to go anything else. Or to do anything else. You could do some things and you couldn't do others, and that's about how it all lined up. Life might lock her into some kind of hell as well. Someday or sooner. No choices, no options, even if she tried her best to be good and clean deep down in her own heart.

A boy stood up on his desk and waved his arms like white wings and then squatted and cawed like a crow. And when she thought of what another minute in that room would do to break what threads of spirit she had left, she slipped out before the teacher had a chance to notice.

Later that day a young man who'd lost half his face and all of his jaw dipping snuff spoke at an assembly in the gymnasium. Worse than his face was his voice, a sound like a gurgle drowning in a bucket of spit.

"Look at me back then," he said and behind him on a big screen appeared his senior prom picture with a pretty blonde girl in a blue gown. He'd been handsome, soft-eyed but with a strong, dimpled chin. All gone now. He didn't have a mustache in the picture and she wondered if he'd grown it to hide the folds and scars of his mutilation.

"But take a good look at me now," he said. "I thought only old people got cancer from dipping and smoking. Old people who smoked and dipped fifty years. Only took me four."

The rest of the students fixed and rigid in the bleachers. Not moving and not speaking and sickened into shock. Now a picture of his hospital room, tubes shoved into his mouth and his nose and his eyes swollen shut and tubes sticking out of his cheeks.

"I'm awful-looking forever," he said, pointing up at the picture behind him and then at his own face. "There's nothing that can fix me now."

More pictures. Faces mangled by tobacco cancer so badly they hardly looked like faces at all. Disasters missing chins and tongues and noses under flat defeated eyes.

"I'm never going to look handsome ever again," he said. "And I look at you and see so many beautiful young people. And I look out at all of you and I know you're hurting yourself. Please," he said. "Quit and keep your beauty. Whatever hole you got in your heart. Don't fill it with dip and cigarettes and dope and liquor. Fill that hole with love."

The students had a chance to ask questions, but she didn't want to hear his answers. She wanted a cigarette and left to search the school for a place to smoke it. Had they buried her dead babies in the same place they'd buried the rest of his face? And now his face had become their faces and they'd visit her gurgling and deformed in her dreams and tell her to quit and keep her beauty. She couldn't sit through another class. Not today. Never again. She wandered the empty walkways and across the place they called the quad. A set of sprinklers shot off and sprayed her with a cold blast of water that smelled like rotten eggs. Pointed fences along the edges of the property she knew she could never climb.

She dried herself off in the empty bathroom and when she came out somebody said, "I see you, young lady."

It was a security guard with a radio clipped to his chest.

"What class you supposed to be in?" he asked her.

She fumbled with the schedule she'd stuck in her back pocket and ran her shaking finger down the grid to the hour.

"Biology," she said.

"Why you so scared?"

"I'm not."

"You're shaking worse than a seizure. What are you hiding? Go ahead and open that backpack."

She set it down by her feet and pulled the zipper open.

"Anything in there that's going to stick me? Needles, knives?"

"No."

He found her cigarettes and held them up and wiggled them and shook his head. "No way," he said. "I'm allowed to smoke these, but you are not. They're even my brand! I thank you. Catch you again it's Dean Markelz and detention. Now get to class."

Through the classroom window she saw the teacher behind his desk reading a newspaper and the students at the high biology tables sleeping on their backpacks and a few girls writing nasty notes decorated with purple highlighters. Nobody cared to notice her enter. The only seat left was next to a pair of girls in black eye makeup who looked like they were actually working. They had a tray beside the table sink. There was a yellow corn snake in the tray and the girls had little scalpels with black handles. And when she squinted into the tray, she saw that the girls were busy butchering the snake down to a pile of bloody waste. They were giggling.

"What the hell are you doing that for?" she asked them.

"We tried to do it right, but we fucked it all up. Who cares?"

"Yeah," the other girl said. "What the fuck do you care?"

At the end of the day she found the same group of Mexican girls who'd packed themselves around the bathroom mirror that morning. They were chewing gum and glaring at the traffic of students leaving the school. She dropped her backpack and walked right up to them and said, "How come you dress like a bunch of nasty whores?"

She turned eighteen in the hospital but her father didn't tell her happy birthday when he drove her home two days later. He only said, "You did this to yourself on purpose. So you wouldn't have to go anymore."

The coyotes calling through the window beside his bed. Calling to wake him so he could catch her ripping him off. But they didn't wake him.

I'm sorry, Daddy.

I know you were trying to help.

Don't come looking for me. No matter what.

I'm nothing worth finding.

2

He didn't need to look to know she was already gone. The skank walk through the waste of the West. The bruised and sutured face in a half look he could see his own. Her thumb out. Motels with nosebleed spots on the pillows and colorless sheets the canvas for a thousand ejaculations. Overpasses, on-ramps, exits. Purple on a toilet stinking the room up worse by the minute. Squatting in the weeds. Popping quarters into Indian casino slots. Brass knuckles flashing from a back pocket and bloody plugs of cotton in her nostrils. Worms, sores, infections, gangrene. The brain pan a clanging alarm of perfect lunacy. Liquor and sink amphetamines both bolts slowing to a crawl of gradual cracks across a ceiling of clouds. Just enough for a cold bottle of gas station wine. A freight train roaring through the frosted cooler glass and dragging you down the tracks the next morning. Ribs like fingers squeezing your chest.

He moved from room to room whispering her name and squinting out the windows. He looked in her closet and under her bed then in his own closet and under his bed. Her name a short echo through the empty house.

In the backyard he stood over the place where he'd buried King. You heard about whores getting murdered all the time. They wound up in dumpsters and ditches. Room to room and window to window. No road was the right road. The insect wicked. The night and whatever it brought.

The first blue of sunrise had leaked into the sky when the taxi rolled up and the driver asked where she was headed.

"Greyhound station. San Bernardino."

He got a good look at her face in his rearview and spun around. "The hell happened to you?"

"Got my ass kicked by some Mexican girls."

She kept looking back at the house and the sky was brightening. "Can we go?"

He studied the garbage bag on the seat beside her, the backpack in her lap. He looked at her face again and said, "You running away from home?"

She reached the five twenties over the seat and waved them and said, "You can't run away if you're eighteen, and I've got the cash so let's go."

When she took out the bottle of hospital Percocet and popped the cap and swallowed two the driver pulled over. "No drugs," he said.

"They're prescribed. Look at me. I just got out of the hospital."

"All right, I'm sorry," he said, then drove on.

"How much is it going to cost me to get to the Greyhound?"

"It's kind of far."

"I know it's far. I asked you how much it's going to cost."

"Twenty bucks."

"Shit."

"You got twenty bucks?"

"What the hell did I just show you?"

She didn't know how much she was supposed to tip him but when she asked him to break a twenty he turned it down and told her she'd need it a lot more than he would.

She broke the twenty inside the station and got five dollars in quarters and called her mother.

"Why in the hell should I speak to you after what you told

your father about me?"

"I'm sorry, Mama."

"You know that telling those kinds of lies could've gotten my ass thrown in jail for child abuse?"

"Please just listen to me. I'm sober. I've been clean for over a week. You can call and ask him."

"A week? Before it was two months, then one month, and it never matters. Then all over again. A week. Jesus, Tammy."

"I want to come home."

"No way."

"Please. I have to."

"No."

"Please."

"Why?"

"I don't belong here. I need to come home to you."

"Is he drinking again?"

"No. But I need money for a bus ticket."

"Why didn't you ask him?"

"He doesn't even know I'm gone. Not yet."

"What are you running from?"

"He wants me to go to this school. Or else he's going to throw me out. And these Mexican girls beat my ass so bad they put me in the hospital. You can call him and ask him. I'm not lying. But I need to come home. Please. I need a ticket."

"Jesus damn Christ, Tammy. How much do you need?"

"A hundred."

Two hours later the cash was waiting at the Western Union window. She didn't buy a ticket.

The streets were Sunday morning dead. She hunched under the burden of her garbage bag luggage. Two more blocks and a magical convergence of luck. A neon open sign in a liquor store's window and nearing the store a bum pushing a shopping cart stuffed with a sleeping bag and a stack of ragged clothes topped with two battered pairs of black sneakers.

She crossed the street and said, "Hey, man. I'll give you five bucks if you buy me some vodka and Marlboros."

He shook his head without looking at her.

"How about ten?"

He stood in the middle of the bus terminal with his hand on the back of his neck, turning. Newspaper racks, candy machines, a closed sign over the empty snack bar. He glanced a few mournful times at the empty bench where he had first seen her.

It was late morning when he got home and called the sheriff's department to report a runaway. He was waiting in the road when the deputy arrived. He asked Weldon how long his daughter had been gone. And then her date of birth.

"November fourth," he said and his knees buckled and his chest went stiff. "1971."

"November fourth was just two days ago."

"I guess so."

"She's not a runaway."

The deputy set his clipboard on the hood and like Weldon stuck his hands in his pockets and looked up at the sky and then down the road to the base of the rocky rise where it ended.

"You can start calling her friends," the deputy said. "I bet you she's with one of them."

"She doesn't have any friends."

"None?"

"None. Neither do I."

Nights she faced many mirrors and nights she needed fewer layers of makeup to hide the bruises that faded and the sutures that fell away on their own. She measured how much makeup checking her reflection in bathrooms and behind bartenders and as she sauntered to the stage twirling through fog and flashing strobes and Guns N' Roses and at the end of rolled fives stuck over fat rails in that moment before she closed her eyes and snorted them up into the damaged vacuum of her face until her brain turned clit twitching with fuck. This week the garage in Grandpa Lady's house where there sat a bed and under a wall of tools the baby's crib and the old woman crowing, "Darna, mind you don't forget the baby's sippy cup. It's been out in the car for three days and the milk has long gone rotten."

The baby's teeth had just come in and they were already brown with bottle rot.

"Darna, don't you think it's high time you found work? Heard they're hiring at Sacaton Cotton."

Midnight on their night off Grandpa Lady raised the garage door and shined a flashlight on them all and the baby screamed and Darna pitched the pipe and the crank under the pillow and the old woman yelled, "I'm your granny, that's all. I don't know what more you want from me."

"Go back to bed."

"I won't. That's it, Darna. I got to put you out. Your friend too. And the baby. All of you."

The baby secured in her stroller and they headed out in the midnight chill of the dry flat air. The stroller jostled over potholes and chunks of what once had been pavement. Squat shit shack houses and yards overgrown with punk brittlebush.

She asked Darna why they couldn't have taken Grandpa Lady's car.

"You fucking kidding me?" Darna bellowed. Her voice woke up dogs trapped behind fences and frightened the child to tears.

"Quit it," Darna told the baby. "Quit."

And then she said, "I got two warrants out. Failure to appear. Maricopa County and Pinal County."

Tammy knew better than to ask what she'd done.

"I'm so fucked," Darna whispered. "If I had as many dicks sticking out of me as I do in me, I'd look like a dick porcupine."

She halted and let loose a harsh sound that was an eruption of weeping. She held out her hands in the manner of lifting an infant who had somehow failed to appear.

* * *

He found himself crossing and re-crossing the same intersections where the fruit of human trade was harvested by razors and cheap pistols. The curbs where scabbed and ragged whores sauntered and hitchhiked in a manner of seductive leisure. An abandoned strip mall and a boarded former grocery store. By the bruises that purpled her face she'd be easy to describe. He asked a few whores if they'd seen her. They walked off with a laugh and a curse of seething annoyance. He stood at the counter inside Jackpot Liquor and the man at the register said, "You beat her up?"

"No, no. She's my daughter."

"That don't mean nothing. Bet you're trying to find her before she goes to the cops."

"Mister."

"She really your daughter or some toy rubber twat climbed into your car?"

"Wait."

"Wait the fuck for what?"

"She's my daughter and she's hurt bad."

"I sell liquor and I sell beer and I sell wine. I got nothing else to ring up and bag. Count the hope you still have, Papa Man. My daughter died of stomach cancer in 1983. Ten years old."

There was a short line of three waiting behind him and he left without saying another word.

He peered through the windshield at the wobbling transients cloaked in greasy blankets and cluttered at bus stops and moving their arms up and down like wings on sick pigeons, the rambling enraged shaking their heads and yelling at his truck as he passed. He drove through the wall of dawn, the streetlights dimming as another light dimmed inside him.

She'd been sitting at the back of McDonald's for over an hour, sneaking slugs of vodka from the bottle in her backpack when the manager finally kicked her out. When he had to ask her a second time the booze rage rose in her face and she stood and said, "Go on and eat your own shit. Eat shit."

He told her he was calling the police and she gathered her backpack and garbage bag and swung them so close to hitting the man that he yelped. She ambled out the door, wavering, to the high sunlight that had burned off the chill and made her feel greasy with sweat.

More traffic. She wasn't sure how far she was from the bus station, but aches thrummed in her legs and made her feel like she'd already been walking a week. She crossed railroad tracks, passed two gas stations, a grocery store, and a transmission repair garage, where she stopped and lit a cigarette and sat on the sidewalk to rest against her bags and try to figure out what to do next. The buzz had withered down to a dizzy fatigue behind her eyes. She stuck the cigarette in her mouth and pulled the backpack onto her lap and a rush cracked her open when she found she'd left the bottle back at McDonald's.

Her feet swelled and the sweat salt burned in the stitched gash that ran across her eyebrow. Before she went in she reached into her backpack for the Percocet bottle. She didn't remember having the last one, but somewhere along the way she had.

There were three long lines waiting to order. She'd forgotten the horror of her face until she noticed them staring. She turned to leave. When she stopped and turned again they were still watching her and she was too ashamed to ask them what the hell they were looking at. She spotted the manager scurrying between the drive-up window and some registers. She wedged herself to the front of the line and said, "Hey, mister. Excuse me, mister."

When he saw her his face went white and wilted. "You've got to leave. I told you I'd call the cops and this is the last time."

"Can I have my bottle back?"

"I threw it out. Now go."

"Come on, man."

She felt the press of even more staring. Jokes and laughter behind her. Her sorry bags and her face battered like a makeup kit of Halloween gore.

"And don't come back."

She glared against the sunlight coming off the passing traffic. Sunday morning would never slip her what she needed. She was afraid to find out how much a motel would cost. Two hundred bucks sizzled down to ashes just as soon as you got them. The smell inside McDonald's had made her pretty hungry and the now the sunlight made her want something cold to drink. A Mountain Dew or a Coke and a bag of cheddar Combos. Or a corndog if they had it. But as she walked a few blocks there was no sign of any place where she might buy them. She felt the end of her strength piss out the bottom of her feet.

Some girls could live this way. Most of them had to. Eating like rats and cleaning themselves like rats. Twitching and biting like rats. While she couldn't even keep track of her vodka. She had to go back to Hufford. He'd be furious about the money, but at least she'd have something to give back. She'd send her mother every cent as well. They'd be happy she was safe. Some girls could live this way. There was always someone to give them chunks of crack and crank. Someone with money. Always someone with money. You had to do things for it. You had to do everything they told you.

An older man in shaded glasses with hair down over his collar and a growth of gray whiskers. He appeared in his taxi as soon as she opened her eyes. The driver biting his nails and waiting by the curb as though she'd called. When she got in and saw how old he was, older than even her father, she knew it wouldn't take much to get something out of him and decided not to go back.

"Where you headed?"

"I need a motel. Something cheap. A bucket. I don't really care how dirty it is as long as it has a bed and a toilet."

"Just make sure you don't sleep in the toilet and piss on the bed."

She put her head back and half laughed. She couldn't help it. He looked pleased with himself for making her laugh. It actually took her a while to settle down. She got her breath back as she stretched herself in the comfort of cold air and the lulling roll of the tires beneath her. She let her head rest on the back of the seat, yawned and then breathed through her nose.

"You know," he said. "Some folks might call you a runaway." He turned in his seat at a stop light and studied her. "But I think you're more like a running-to. Like you're running to something. You see what I'm saying?"

He reached his hand over the back of the seat and introduced himself with a name that sounded like Petty Car Thief.

"Petty what?"

"Petty Carthy. Now think about this. What is it you running to?"

"I don't really know. I haven't thought about it much."

He looked into the rearview, squinting through his tinted lenses and pointed at her in the reflection and chuckled. "I see you sneaking around back there. Must be up from around Sneakyville. Am I right?"

"Can you just let me out up here at the Chevron station?"

"I didn't mean anything by that."

"Let me out, man."

He did, his face white silence itself with thin lips and a twitch in his cheek.

"How much do I owe you?"

"Four dollars if you know how to ride in a cab."

She stood on the pavement with a bag in each hand. She dropped them. A man at one of the pumps watched her and continued to watch once he'd hung the nozzle back up and twisted his gas cap closed and shut the hatch. Petty Carthy's taxi rolled away.

"Wait!" she yelled. She jumped in place and waved her arms.

"Stop!"

She shut the door and he shook his head and whistled through his teeth once and laughed. They pulled onto a freeway and Petty Carthy asked, "What is it happened to your pretty face?"

"Got beat up."

"Beat up?"

"Mexican girls."

"They just come up and jump you on the street?"

"School."

"They sure worked you over."

"I kind of asked for it."

"I know what you mean. I'm asking for it every time I get behind the wheel. I been spit in the face, stabbed, shot in the shoulder, blackjacked and sapped until my brains leak out my ears. Been pushed out of my own cab at thirty miles an hour. Been kidnapped."

"How long you been driving?"

"Two weeks," he said. Then he slapped the wheel and cackled at himself and said, "Fifteen years, Miss Running-To. And fifteen years of anything will sure as shit paint your picture."

They exited the freeway and turned onto an avenue of chain linked auto shops for tires, mufflers, and transmissions. A check cashing place and a boot place and a discount cigarette place. Her mind found the right words for easing into asking for vodka.

"Loneliness is about the worst thing in the world," she said.

"Maybe. I know there are worse things than that. But I'd put lonely times up there for sure."

"I've been the loneliest I've ever felt over the last two months. But I don't know how to get out of it except for drinking."

"I'll drink to that," Petty Carthy said. He lifted a bottle of something brown out from under his seat and took two gulps.

When he screwed the cap on and stuck the bottle back under his seat, she almost asked him to let her out so she wouldn't waste any more money.

"Sitting on the couch watching television," she said.

"Drinking, smoking weed, just anything to get out of that loneliness."

"Until your folks caught you."

"My dad."

"Well shit a brick on that party."

"Mister, I was wondering if you could get me some vodka."

He squinted his eyes so tight one of them closed and he hummed a sound in the back of his throat like a child hiding under a blanket and crying.

"Mister Petty Carthy can get his ass in a whole lot of deep shit buying a runaway running-to booze."

"I've got the money."

"I know you do."

And once she had that bottle between her legs there was no longer a destination. Petty Carthy kept his bottle on the floorboard and they both cracked their windows and lit cigarettes. The liquor went to her head, a rolling ball of pulsing silver.

"The dark still scares me, no matter how old I get," she said.

"I never liked driving down roads with no signs."

"Something might jump out at you. A face with a beard and mean eyes."

"Nobody likes hitting a dead end. Daylight or midnight."

"The dark on the inside is worse than the dark on the outside. Walls and corners in the dark, they're places you can't get out of. But you can see a field in the dark once your eyes get used to it. You can always find some kind of light out there. But the only light inside is the one inside your brain that wants to shine all over the things you don't want to see."

"I don't exactly own this taxi but nobody can take it away from me. Not as long as I have anything to say about it. Or do about it. I get wind of that and I'll drive down to Mexico by way of the state of Arizona. Or New Mexico down to Old Mexico. Maybe even as far as Texas and then down and boom I'm a Mexican and nobody can have my cab."

"Sometimes when I wake up I expect it to be morning but

then all the windows are just black and sometimes when I expect to wake up in the dark the worst kind of light's just blasting through the windows."

"No man's a whole man if he can get the floor of his livelihood yanked right out from under him like a trick rug. Like the Three Stooges."

"It's the worst kind of light because it shows all the sins you collected in the dark."

"You can see your own sins whether it's light out or dark. When it's light, your sins cast a million shadows all over you. And when it's dark, your sins light up in a gradual heat. First as embers twitching in your heart, then as fire right out of your eyes. You can't put them out. Nothing can. Sin sticks to you until you're a roaring log they put in the ground."

"Can we go find some methamphetamine?"

Mister Petty Carthy told her that he could indeed round her up some methamphetamine. "We just need to go locate my soul brother at the swap meet. Shake and Bake. Shake and Bake sells knives and swords."

"And crank?"

"And crank."

She didn't remember finishing the first bottle but there it lay on the floor by her foot and now a new one on her knee. The afternoon had fallen into a hand of pink streaks waving goodbye.

"Let's put some head music back into your head."

She slammed her door and leaned against it and said, "Give me a second," and tipped the bottle.

"Hey, hey," Petty Carthy whispered. He pulled the bottle from her and hid it between them. "Goddamn, keep this in the car. And you want me to get you some speed?"

"Aw, man."

"Keep shut of that 'Aw, man.' I should have known better than to pick you up. Between the bags and the cuts and the black eyes. I should have known."

He leaned down and got close to her face. "How the hell old

are you, anyway?"

"I'm fine. Fine."

"I've seen cops in there sometimes."

A stuffy wind of popcorn nacho funnel cake cotton candy churros. She had to amble sideways a few steps until she stopped herself by grasping a trash can.

"Christ almighty," Petty Carthy said. "You going to puke? Shit," he said. "You're going to vomit your guts."

"No."

She ground her teeth through her wants. She was scared her drunk might fade. They followed the lagging crowds who stopped at the booths to admire used tools, mirrors frosted with skeletons and unicorns, toy dogs who could bark and flip, fuzzy red floorboard rugs, steering wheels made out of chains, antique garbage laid out on tarps spread over sections of cracked blacktop.

Another hot popcorn stink and her mood turned even darker. "These people move slower than cripples."

"They're shopping."

The blacktop with booths on either side crowded with legs and feet and stroller wheels. She allowed the distortions of oncoming faces. Fat kids, country and Mexican, stuffing themselves with cotton candy. She wanted a cigarette but had left them in the taxi so she had to ask Petty Carthy for one.

"No," he told her.

"Why not?"

"The more you give to people, the more they take."

She rolled her eyes and sighed.

"I been driving you all over the wide world. Getting your liquor for you. Now I'm giving you a guided tour all the way to snort. Now you want my cigarettes."

She spotted a display of musical instruments. Drums, horns, microphone stands. Amplifiers and guitars. She shouldered her way through the crowds to see them. A father with his teenage son were running the booth. They looked at her with a gaze of stunned disgust.

"Can I try that guitar?" she asked.

"Test drives are for paying customers."

"I got money. You think I don't have money?" She reached into her pocket and pulled out the cash. "Well I do have money. See? See it?"

A strange voice deep and tall behind her told her to step back. He took her arm and she went rigid because she knew there were two cops standing behind her.

"You've been drinking."

"Where'd you get all this cash?"

She saw Petty Carthy strolling along the displays with his hands behind his back. He'd abandoned her. She didn't bother calling his name.

"I said where's you get all this money? You hustling? Your booster beat your little ass?"

"No," she said. "My mother wired it to me this morning. From Oklahoma. I got it at the station in San Bernardino."

"What station was that?"

"Bus station. Greyhound."

"How much have you had to drink?"

"I haven't been drinking."

"Don't you lie to me. How old are you?"

"Twenty-one."

Worry turned first in her head then spiraled through her stomach. Her bags, her clothes, her makeup. Her vodka.

"You got any ID?"

They had her in handcuffs and were leading her out.

"What did I do? I didn't do nothing."

They stuck her in the back of a cruiser.

"What's your name?"

"Tammy."

"Tammy what?"

"Tammy Holt."

"Where do you live?"

"Hufford."

"Where's your car?"

"Don't have a car."

"How'd you get here?"

"Took a cab."

She expected them to be writing things down, but they weren't. They were watching the families walk past who looked in the windows when they saw her in the back.

"You smell like a liquor store, you know that? And I don't think you're twenty-one."

"No," the other one said. "You sure as hell aren't twenty-one." He didn't turn around. It looked like he was talking to the steering wheel. "I don't know what the hell kind of scrap you got into. And I don't care. And I don't think you took any goddamn cab all the way from Hufford to go to a swap meet. But I don't honestly care about that either. What I do care about is some little girl here hustling her little ass with children around. And what I also care about is you lying right into my ears."

"I'm not lying."

"Shut your goddamn mouth. I'm driving you to the exit and that's sure for shit what you're going to do. Exit. I don't want to see you hustling your little ass around here again."

They let her out and told her to walk. Told her to take her little hustling money and her little hustling ass back to wherever she'd come from.

She turned around once and saw them both sitting there on the edge of the parking lot watching her. She walked for over an hour and passed a beauty salon with sun-faded hairstyle posters of Mexican girls in the windows that made her whole face throb. She looked away and faced the sidewalk ahead of each step. Then she passed an equipment yard. Spikes up through her feet and her ankles thick in her shoes. She stopped once and bent over and squeezed the strain in her calves. Then even less traffic and soon no businesses to see. Streets turned to roads and on either side ranges of scrub and mesquite trees and chunks of rubble concrete and lengths of rusted twisted rods and broken bottles and flattened hamburger bags and big plastic cups with pictures of superheroes trying with fierce might to fly away from them. They found girls in places like this. Naked and strangled and rotting.

The hour pushed the very last of the daylight down behind a short range of hills torn across the bottom of the sky. Half a chill and then a full chill blew through the sky. Her walk a pace that pressed the earth until the earth was again sidewalk that led her past the beauty salon and its posters of beautiful dark eyes watching her pass.

The cops were gone and aside from a few cars the only thing left of the lot was the white gravel and dust spread across it. When she spotted Petty Carthy's cab her chest almost split open. She ran to it and cupped her face and looked in the back window and saw the vodka bottles on the floorboard and her bags on the seat.

The swap meet itself was somehow still open but the stalls and booths were all but empty. No more music. No more crowds lumbering along through the dirty air of fried shit. She passed the music display where she'd been taken away. The instruments were gone but the father and son were still there taping and stacking boxes. The father was saying to his son, "Answer me. Answer me."

She followed the path around the bend and there she saw Petty Carthy standing next to a table. Behind it was a broad bearded man with flat strands of hair oiled across his scalp wearing eyeglasses stained green with cigarette smoke.

"Go on," Petty Carthy said when he saw her. "You got cop stink all over you."

"He your friend?"

"I said go on."

"I am his friend," the man behind the table announced. He was standing behind a set of three tables covered with a display of daggers, pocketknives, hunting knives, Bowie knives, throwing knives, knight swords, even Oriental swords. The kind up on the wall in Oriental restaurants. She wanted to touch them, but he was wrapping them all up. Below the tables hung both an American flag and a Dixie flag.

"I truly am Shake and Bake," he said, smiling even as he smoked. She knew it was a menthol cigarette by the end of the green pack sticking out of his T-shirt pocket. "You must be Petty Carthy's friend Sugar Girl."

"I said go on," Petty Carthy said, and Shake and Bake waved him off.

"Heard you got busted down on Bourbon Street. Must've blasted your way out of the jail just like Calamity Jane. Bang bang!" he said, guns at his hips with his fingers.

She asked him if she could get a cigarette. She could have crawled up under the Dixie flag to sleep.

"As long as you don't mind a menthol."

"Don't give her one. I said get out and go on with your cop stink."

"You're paranoid," Shake and Bake said. "Old and paranoid."

Petty Carthy wrinkled his face and crossed his arms and looked at the ground.

They loaded all the boxes into Petty Carthy's trunk. She reached down for the vodka and Shake and Bake told her to pass it up front but she handed him the empty by mistake and he laughed and said, "Earth to Calamity Sugar Girl," in a squeaky robotic voice that made him hoot.

After another mile Shake and Bake produced a white baggy and scooped out a bump with the end of a key and held it over the seat and both headlights and taillights flashed in his glasses and it was like looking straight into a face of lightning. He finally turned away when she was wiping her nose with the back of her hand and fixed up a key for Petty Carthy, who snorted and called out, "God almighty!"

"You like to feel good?" Shake and Bake asked her.

"Who doesn't?"

"That's right. Got to feel good in a feel bad world."

"That's a life lesson to live by," Petty Carthy said.

Shake and Bake put his arm over the backseat and looked at her over his green glasses. "What makes you feel good?"

"Whatever makes me happy, I guess."

He took a deep breath and looked across the seat at Petty Carthy and said, "What makes you happy, Petty?"

"Oh, let's see. Hamburgers with onions. French fries with gravy. Cigarettes, haircuts. Nice new clothes. Western clothes with pearly snaps and fancy designs."

He put his arm back over the seat and asked her if parties made her feel good.

"Depends on who's there."

"Pooh Bear, Soft Serve, Franklin, Rock n' Roll, Papers, Cheeks, Chowder, Chink, Danny Dare, and Linda Zipp. More than that but I don't know who all."

She squeezed her arms around herself and pressed her back as deeply into the seat as she could.

"Why you so nervous, Sugar Girl?"

"I'm not."

"Nothing's going to happen to you except for feeling good."

"Feeling good's good enough for me," said Petty Carthy. He'd reached under his seat for his bottle and turned it up until the last of it was gone. He handed it to Shake and Bake, who rolled down the window and pitched it out to the night. She turned to watch it smash but saw nothing over the dark and heard nothing over the engine.

They exited to a road called Limonite. Warehouses and stacks of hay underneath shelters. More warehouses and a barn and railroad tracks and another barn. A corral where two horses in blinders stood facing one another with their heads hanging. It looked like they were breaking up.

Shake and Bake took a bump off the key into both sides of his nose. He coughed into his fist, rubbed his face with both hands, then groaned and said to Petty Carthy, "Hey, if you were sentenced to death, what would you request for your execution dinner?"

"My what?"

"Your last meal. They'll give you anything you ask for before they turn on the gas?"

"I don't really know. I haven't thought about it."

"Well think about it."

"All right. Fried chicken."

"What else?"

"Onion rings."

"And?"

"And ice cream and vanilla pudding and a can of peaches."

"Hope they give you a diaper before they strap you in."

A few little houses on either side of a dirt road which was rutted and studded with stones.

"Know what I want for my last meal?" Shake and Bake asked.

"What?" said Petty Carthy.

"The guard whose job it is to turn on the gas!"

He laughed and clapped and bounced in his seat and shook the entire body and filled the car with a ringing nightmare hysteria.

They pulled up to a house at the end of the road and the front door was open and some folks were standing around it, smoking and taking tugs of bottles of beer and Petty Carthy said, "Well at least they're doing some home drinking tonight."

"Take out a goddamn loan once you get that tab at Applebee's. Come on, Sugar Girl. Just leave your shit here."

The way they hugged and yelled and gripped their fists, the men inside hadn't seen Petty Carthy and Shake and Bake for twenty years. But then everyone was wasted and when you're wasted you'll dive into a pile of horseshit in flames. She felt them all watching her through foggy stares. She was too busy looking for liquor to care. Everyone else had a drink. Bottles and cans or both. But she'd been straight for too long now. Sick sober when the drunk leaves your gut and sticks its claws out trying to pull itself back in with a scraping need. The head kick of Shake and Bake's crank had lasted all of fifteen minutes. Garbage cut with Comet. Dish soap drip down the back of her throat.

"And this here is Sugar Girl."

When they called her their voices rose and fell in a strain of childlike hospitality. The house was as big as her father's. Poor and small. She moved through it searching. She found a six pack of Coors Silver Bullets in the sink and gunned two and the rest of the party forgot she was there.

"You know him. Peewee, that faggot taxi driver who drives blind old ladies to church."

"No shit. How?"

"Shotgun."

"No shit. Never would have thought he had a shotgun."

"You knew him?"

"Knew of him."

"Then how the hell would you have considered whether or not he had a shotgun?"

"His name. Peewee. And that he's a faggot. Or was a faggot."

Shake and Bake was making his way toward the refrigerator with his arm around a bald little man in plastic glasses. "If you were sentenced to death, what would you request to eat for your execution dinner?"

"No death penalty in California."

"Arizona, New Mexico, Texas."

"Corn," he said.

"Corn?"

"Corn on the cob."

"With butter and salt?"

"You bet."

"I can see it," Shake and Bake said. "Know what I want for my last meal?"

She got tired of standing and took the last four cans out of the sink. The table in the corner was covered with piles of yellowed newspapers and rusted tools and auto parts caked with black grease. There was one chair and she took it and sat the cans in her lap and opened another one and drank until she felt the first two finally tingle on through the middle of her forehead to the back of her skull.

"They closed the Magnolia plasma bank six months ago. Where the hell you been, man?"

"Out at the San Bernardino County farm, you dandy ass candy ass motherfucker."

"Where's Pooh Bear? Anyone seen Pooh Bear?"

"He took Papers and Cheeks out for cigarettes."

"Pooh Bear shouldn't be driving any damn place. He shouldn't even be allowed to drive a play baby wagon."

"He'll end up his ass in Presley Detention."

"Elvis can steam up his asshole."

Laughter stuffed the house louder than a box of rubber birthday dogshit.

"He fixed that Vacu-Flow 560 and it broke a week later."

"Don't he work for Bob Milky at the Pyrite garage?"

Milky fired him and now he's shoveling shit at a boarding stable off Limonite. Do you know what he said about his own sister? I know her and it's true. Bullshit. True shit. That lawnmower was mine by right and by fact. You don't even have a lawn. What the fuck do you care? Well that shit heel's going to get it in his eye. Get what? It, fool. He's going to get it in the eye. It? It? If you don't understand I'm not going to learn you. Well how many other times did the landlord take their baby? I heard he used a rope. He used rope for his hands but the power cord for the noose. How come Soft Serve became a pastor when he didn't even finish high school? For one, he's just a youth pastor. A youth pastor for the retarded children. Any old fool can preach. You can preach if you're blind. Hell, they love it when you're blind.

"You don't look so good."

She blinked and wiped an eye with the back of her hand. He had yellow teeth under an orange mustache. Cut off his head and he'd make the ugliest pumpkin on the block.

"You drink all these yourself?"

"I don't know."

"You're pale."

"Most white people are."

He put his head back and his shoulders shook and he laughed without making a sound.

"Who's white? I'm only part-time white and full-time fool. Watch this."

She didn't watch anything but sensed his wavering dance in the tight space behind her. She moved the sliding door aside and slipped out back where a few men sat around a firepit of cardboard garbage and plywood scraps stuffed inside a wheel well. She didn't know where her cigarettes had gone. Then she found a whole unopened pack of Salems in her back pocket. She couldn't find a lighter and since she didn't care what they'd see in her face or say when they saw it she went over to the fire and the three men said hello and she nodded back and took the end of a plywood plank and brought the flaming up and held it to her Salem and puffed until it ignited and one of them said, "Easy there," and she shrugged and put the plank into the fire and went back to the patio of cracked cement and stood under the light and smoked. It tasted like smoking a whole box of mints.

When she looked through the door glass she saw Petty Carthy and Shake and Bake dancing together like a man and a woman and everyone around them clapping. Then more cheers of welcome. Pooh Bear, Papers, Cheeks, Soft Serve, Shenton, Franklin, Danny Dare. Men squeezed up against the door glass, dirty shirt after dirty shirt, sag ass after sag ass. More shirts squeezed up to the kitchen windows. She held her foot up and ground the Salem against the bottom in a shower of orange sparks then stomped her foot and flicked the dead filter in the yard.

She knocked on the glass to get back inside but nobody heard her. A longhaired man in big purple sunglasses threw up on the kitchen windows and called to the men by the fire.

"The kitchen is closed, gentlemen. The food is gone. There are no more egg salad sandwiches to speak of. There is no bread to speak of and there is no egg salad to speak of."

"Go make a run."

"The grocery stores are finished for the evening as well."

"Ralph's is open twenty-four, honey."

"I'm not leaving this house."

"There beer left?"

"There's beer and rum and vodka and various and sundry other spirits."

"Then who gives a fuck about your egg salad?"

Then a scream in the yard. A man had fallen into the fire and the other two men were struggling to pull him out. When they finally lifted him his jacket and a pantleg were burning bright. He tottered toward her with his arms stretched out like Jesus on the run.

She went around the house to the road that passed before it. There were cars parked on both sides. Many more than there had been when she'd arrived. She looked up and down but didn't see Petty Carthy's taxi. She looked again. She felt one last drop of alcohol rolling around inside her head. One drop and nothing more. She felt instead something in herself and of herself there in the middle of the road. Tammy back then and Tammy later on and Tammy now. She noticed the cold and took one last look at all the cars and saw that Petty Carthy's taxi was gone for certain.

At the end of the road a rise of boulders she could shape even in the middle of the night and when she looked down the other end of the road she knew Tammy back then. She looked again at the rise of boulders, a grave for a pile of souls who'd quit the years they'd spent waiting for a promising day that never came and she knew Tammy later on, knew she was somehow back on the road where her father lived just this side of the wash where starving coyotes and night dogs prowled howling, and despite the lights of the party in the house behind her and though her father's name wasn't on the mailbox, she knew it was his house as much as this house was not, but she still cupped her hands over her eyes and peered into her own room to find the radio and television and bed her father had gotten her, but Tammy back then was either gone or hiding behind the shut shades, but she knocked on the front door anyway, first like a visitor, no louder than a tap, then louder, harder, a pair of hammers.

Daddy. Daddy help. Daddy help me. Daddy help me I'm lost. Daddy help me I'm lost and I'm sorry I ripped you off and left.

Then more knocking until she ran out of knuckles and her voice. She staggered into the yard. His truck was gone anyway. She sat on the spot where the yard met the road and waited to see if he'd ever come home. She waited until the party shut down and everyone had left. They all waved to her as they drove by but nobody stopped to see if she needed a lift. None of them. But she followed the last one to leave all the way until his brake lights disappeared.

Tammy back then and Tammy later on didn't tell Tammy now to stop and go back or to keep on walking until some better red brake light luck rolled up and shook her hand to guide her back to the swap meet guitar and a chance to show them all how she could play it and to the vodka McDonald's and a chance to drink it and to that bus station hundred and a chance to blow it and when she checked her back pocket her pack of Salems was gone, her only friend left, and when she checked her front pockets so was the cash her mother had wired and what was left of the money she'd stolen from her father, and her backpack was off somewhere in Petty Carthy's taxi, and so were the rest of her clothes, all the skin she had left once the clothes she was wearing went and decided to rot and fall off.

A trio of prisoners. Tammy later on up front and Tammy back then following behind.

Until both of them broke away and left Tammy now with

her hands stuck in her empty pockets crunch stepping the and the dust along the edge of the road.

Her footsteps echoing all the way to the end of the outside chill and back.

3

And one night he saw her hitchhiking along the curb and she hopped right in as soon as he pulled over. Her eyes bright with caution and behind that caution fury and behind that fury shame. But she wasn't Tammy. She thanked him. She had on a pair of ass shorts and a greasy sweater that hung off a prominent collar-bone. Whatever Walgreens perfume she'd sprayed on didn't hide the sweat dried by the cold night. He hadn't yet pulled away from the curb and she was looking over her shoulder and through the back window for cops. But all of him had sunken into his seat. He still couldn't believe it wasn't her and he didn't have the strength to take the wheel into his hands nor to tell the girl to get out.

"You want to get going, honey?" she said and he nodded and took his foot off the brake.

"You got a cigarette?" she asked.

"No, sorry. I don't smoke."

"Shit," she said. "Well I'll blow you for twenty bucks and let you fuck me for forty."

"No, no," he said. "That's not what I'm looking for."

"You want me to piss on you? Take a shit on you?"

He glanced at her. "No," he said. "None of that."

"Well what the fuck you pick me up for? Just let me out, man."

"Hold on a second."

"No, pull over."

"Let me buy you breakfast."

"I'm not hungry and I got work to do so pull the fuck over and let me out."

"Double your pay. Double you tops."

She crossed her arms and stuck her dirty thumbnail in her mouth. "All right," she said. "You some kind of preacher? Because I don't want to be preached at."

"I'm not a preacher."

"I don't like people judging me."

"I won't."

She shrugged and shook her head and rolled her eyes all at once like a quiet but drastic seizure. "What the hell are you then?"

"What I am is out here looking for my daughter."

"Whatever, man. It's your eighty bucks."

"Eighty bucks," he said.

She turned in her seat to glare at him and said, "You told me double, man. And double's eighty bucks. It's eighty bucks or let me out."

"No, I'll pay you. I promise."

"How do I know?"

He reached back for his wallet and set it on his leg and took out five twenty-dollar bills from the other two hundred he'd brought along.

"Here," he said. "Eighty and twenty more for the tip."

She snatched the bills from him and told him to pull over at a Circle K so she could get some cigarettes. He watched her through the big store windows and under the store's bright lights behind sales posters for cases of Tecate and Bud Light. She looked dirty and too skinny and her lean against the counter was slouched and tired and her oily colorless hair was pulled back into a tail so tight he could see the veins in her temples like worms beneath her skin. The girl stiffened and yelled at the man behind the counter and the tendons in her neck swelled taut. She pushed the door with both hands flat against the glass and stomped back to his truck and got in.

"Motherfucker won't sell me no cigarettes without ID."

"I'm sorry," he said as he looked over his shoulder and shifted into reverse.

"Man, why can't you go in and buy them?"

"Because he saw you get into my truck and he'll see me get out and he'll know I'm buying them for you."

"Can't you at least try?"

He touched the brake and watched her for a second then moved back into the spot and set the truck in park and cut the engine.

"Marlboro reds," she said. "Two packs. Marlboro reds."

He was in the store when he realized he'd left his keys in the ignition. He watched her through the windshield to see if she might scoot across the seat and drive away. But she just stared with a dull-eyed gaze out her window with her thumbnail between her teeth.

The man behind the counter was heavy soft with curly black hair and he smirked and shook his head and said, "I told her no and I'm telling you no. No."

"Come on, buddy."

"Nope."

"You think nicotine is the worst thing she puts in her body?"

"I told you no. Last time. No."

"Last time until what?"

"Until I officially refuse service and call 911."

A strange anger started down at the bottom of his back but in his fatigue it moved no further than needles in his shoulders. He opened his eyes and found his palms flat on the counter. A position for getting frisked. Or the way the girl's hands were flat against the dashboard like she was bracing herself for a head-on.

"How much are Marlboros?"

"Well what difference does that make?"

"I just want to know."

"Two bucks a pack."

"I'll pay you forty for two of them."

The man squinted and scratched his face. He looked out the window at Weldon's truck and so did Weldon and together they regarded the girl who'd drawn up her knees and had both arms wrapped around them and appeared to have fallen asleep. A filthy fetus in a womb of glass and steel who would be reborn a thousand more times onto sidewalks and parking lots in the dark and in the sun and in the blades and in the blood.

"Forty bucks?"

"Forty."

The man crossed his arms and rested them down on the counter close enough to touch Weldon's fingertips. "Getting sucked off depends on it. Don't it?"

"I guess so."

"What if you let me see you jerk yourself off back in the stock?"

"Back in the stock."

"That's all you have to do."

"That's all."

"You could get it up again for that skanky little thing out there."

And then the sound of his own horn. One long moan and the girl's arms outstretched in a display of sophisticated exasperation.

The man straightened and coughed into his hand and took Weldon's money and gave him the cigarettes and turned his back to busy himself with some figures in the clipboard.

She tore open the pack like an animal at candy. She lit one and moaned a little behind the drag and rolled her window down and felt the chill and rolled it back up and soon the inside filled like an aquarium of fog.

After a few blocks he said, "So your going rate is twenty

bucks?"

"I already told you."

"I'm just surprised. I mean to get into a stranger's truck."

"I said I don't like people judging me."

She shook her head, sucked the butt down to the brown end, then cracked the window and flicked it out.

"I don't like this," she said. "Pull over."

"I won't judge you again. All right? I gave you a hundred bucks and got you your cigarettes and now all you have to do is eat breakfast with me."

They took a booth in an all-night coffee shop and the waitress looked the girl over before she gave them menus. The girl didn't need one.

"Scrambled eggs. Bacon and sausage. You got grits? Grits. Toast with butter. And bring grape jelly. And I want a Coke to drink too."

She barely chewed. He didn't think she had all her teeth. Her throat swelled and squeezed in her swallowing like a voluptuous white snake. Her plate was clean and she was licking her fingertips with the quick nibbling manner of a rat when Weldon asked her name.

"Sam," she said. "Short for Samantha. Sometimes they call me Gurgle Girl."

"How old are you?"

"Nineteen."

"How long you been doing this?"

"Here we go."

"Look, I've got a daughter about your age. She left a few weeks ago and I think she's around here."

"Well I haven't seen her."

"How do you know?"

"I'd know a girl if she was working my age. I mean I know one of them but she's been out here over a year and she's black anyway. Is that all you wanted to know?"

"I don't know if she's working or not."

"What the fuck else you think she'd be doing out here?"

"I don't know," he said. "What else is there?"

"To do out here?"

"Yes."

"Besides sucking dick?"

"I guess."

"You get high. You smoke crank or rock. You daughter smoke crank?"

"She does."

"Hey," she said and lowered her face to the top of her folded hands. "Let's score some. Crank. You and me. Talk. We can talk about your daughter."

"I'm lost," he said. "I have so many questions. I'm sorry. I shouldn't do that with you. I need to find her."

The mean shot back into her thin eyes and she snapped up so hard the whole booth shook. "Well I don't know why you're coming to me. I told you I haven't seen her."

"Listen, I have questions about the kind of life you live. Like where do you stay? Do you get around all over or do you stick around this side of town? You know. On the streets. Where's your family?"

"I don't want to talk about any of that shit."

"How does a girl decide to end up sticking her thumb out to strangers in the middle of the night?"

"I don't want to talk about that shit either. That isn't your business no matter how much cash you throw at me."

"Hold on."

"I ate with you. That was the deal." She scooted across the booth and stood up. "Take me back to where you found me."

They passed a one-floor apartment complex divided by a row of dead shrubs from a lot and garage and office house for truck rentals. Beside that an empty strip mall and then a Church of God of Prophecy. No streetlights. No headlights oncoming or behind or passing. Just night and its folds of turns and shadows. For the first time since he'd picked her up, the girl was at peace.

Her legs crossed and the smoke curling around her form like reverent burning spices offered for a young holy bride.

"What if your own father came looking for you?"

"What if he did?"

"Would you go back home with him?"

"One, he wouldn't come looking for me because he doesn't even know where the hell I am and he's up in bumfuck Colorado. And two, I wouldn't go back with him even if he did come looking, because now I'd be sleeping with a knife under my pillow for when he sneaks in to see me late at night."

"But pretend he wasn't like that. And what if he came to help you."

She tilted her head and the muscles in her face relaxed as if readying herself to smile. "You're probably wasting your time looking for your daughter," she said. "And look at her," she said and pointed at a big black whore in heels wobbling down the sidewalk with her thumb out. "That nasty ass bitch has worms in her pussy," she said. She wheeze-laughed and slapped her knee and pitched her cigarette out the window.

She couldn't stop laughing for some time and her laughter sucked at something wet in the back of her lungs. When she finally caught her breath she let out a sigh and said, "Go on and drop me off at that Food City. Around back."

He pulled his truck along the empty docks behind the store where the semis would park and where the drivers would push stacks of crates up the ramp on delivery carts. As soon as he put the engine in park, she moved in for him and he caught the flash of the blade the second she hit the switch and pressed just the tip into the side of his neck and he felt his flesh give under the puncture and shock.

"Motherfucker," she said. "Give me that wallet or I'll cut your daughter fucking head off."

His hands were already raised and when he reached around for his pocket the night bloomed with the red-and-blue flashes from the top of a cruiser. The colors stabbing through the glass. The girl ditched the switchblade under the seat before the spotlight filled the cab. They both had to squint.

By the time they were both in handcuffs on opposite sides of the truck, another cruiser had pulled up and the girl was laughing again like a sick bird while a deputy slapped her. All their cash on the hood of the truck and a deputy whistled and asked him how many blow jobs a man could get in one night.

"She tried to rob me," he said. "She stuck me. I'm bleeding. Go ahead and look under the seat."

"I don't care if there's a pot of goddamn gold under your seat, amigo."

They put Weldon in one cruiser and the girl in the other. She'd been laughing the whole time.

"You should have just let me suck your dick, mister. I give the best head in California."

Tucson was two hours south and she wasn't sure if the Buick they'd borrowed off Pooh Bear would make it. She'd only been in Phoenix two months and already one of the girls she ran with was dead. The powerline poles a long row of crosses between the railroad tracks and the interstate. She saw Jesus on every one of them. Jesus from the picture on the wall in his white robes with his arms out. Jesus from the picture on the wall with his beard and blue eyes with his arms out. Jesus from the picture on the wall sitting on a boulder in the sun with all the little children.

They'd all wanted to go to Tucson but there was only room in the Buick for four. Luxury Dawn and Summer Raine and Ruby who drove and Tammy who sat beside her. Dust devils twisted out of the ground and shafts of lightning cracked the afternoon. Every flash made them jump and under the clouds the mountains blocked the deserts from stretching any further. Billboards for The Thing! and Feed the Ostrich! They passed the glass front and back and jabbered a smoke throated gossip punctuated now and then with an outburst of emotion for poor Lady London, whose funeral this afternoon was their destination.

"Told myself I'd never go to another funeral the rest of my life."

"Fawna didn't have no funeral."

"Listen to what I'm saying."

"Who the hell's Fawna?"

"Just listen, listen."

"She was the one they found way out in Apache Junction. Her arms were cut off."

"Good Lord Jesus."

"They never found her arms neither."

"Don't you remember that?"

"I never heard it in the first place."

"Where you been?"

"I've been where I've been. Where I need to be if I want the jukebox to sing and the quarters dropping into my purse."

"Told myself I'd never go to another funeral the rest of my life."

"It's going to be all right, girl."

"Funeral man begged my mama to keep that casket shut."

"She wanted to see him one last time because of how much she loved him I bet."

"Looked like a pizza in a suit. Now that's how I remember him. That's how I'll always remember Daddy."

Tammy flipped the visor down and grimaced at how thin her hair was getting. The sores on her hands were getting nasty. She tried to cover them up with a coat of skin cream, but the sores glared right on through. And for some reason the little rubber bandages made them hurt even worse.

"This radiator blows out and you'll all have to suck a whole rodeo to pay it off."

"Or you'll have to suck Pooh Bear. He's worse than a whole rodeo."

"This John told me about these tigers in Russia. They chase

bears way up into the trees and so the bears have to build nests for themselves. If they don't stay up in their nests the tigers will kill them. Bears. Bears living up in the trees like birds. There's always something stronger than the strongest meanest thing out there."

"I'm a tiger running Pooh Bear up a damn tree."

The AC was shot and the windows were mouths of hot howling and the backseat was a blowing thatch of hair and they squawked over each other and passed the crackling glass and yelled over the gale and when she looked up at the visor again she was sure her hair had already grown back and when she smiled her white pipe burned lip cracked and bled and when they pulled off at Picacho for gas Luxury Dawn helped her out of the car when she saw the blood running down her chin and said, "Now wash that good and clean before it takes the pus."

Summer Raine took her into the toilet and wiped her mouth with tissue off a dusty roll and said, "Kiss it all better now, baby," and ran the tip of her tongue over the cut and sat her up on the sink and ran her tongue deeper until Ruby banged on the door hollering about Luxury Dawn wanting to go to Tucson to see Lady London one last time to give her the respect she deserved.

Her funeral was held in a one-room strip mall church called His Upper Room but she didn't know whose upper room or why it was called an upper room at all when the church had no upstairs. They jostled past one another to make straight for Lady London's casket up front, a staggering heap that ignored Lady London's family seated in the front three rows of plastic chairs, a pair of ancient black women in the last row cooling themselves with gold paper fans.

She'd seen Lady London passed out many times in many places and in many positions, but never dressed as nicely as she was now in a purple dress like the kind a lady might wear to work in an office. Her hands folded, not passed out but sleeping, and not sleeping but deep and dead. Some of the men in her family had stood and they adjusted their jackets while they watched these strange and dirty visitors. She was scared not because the men were black—two others had stood as well—but because they were angry.

Ruby fell to her knees and Luxury Dawn and Summer Raine both called out and bent to lift her up. "It's too much," she said. "I can't take seeing her laid up and dead. Dead, dead, dead."

A few men came over to help but when they got to the casket, they asked the four women to leave.

Ruby cried and said, "She was the queen of us all. She was queen of the streets. Lady London!"

"Her name was Elizabeth. Her name was not Lady London. Now please get out. All of you."

"A real lady. Lady London."

"How dare you?"

The two old women watched the girls leave and for a moment they stilled their golden fans so as not to miss a second of commotion.

They stood on the sidewalk, smoking for a while before they noticed they'd gone from four down to three. Ruby was missing. Back to Phoenix with Pooh Bear's Buick. The life dropped out of their bodies like babies slapping the pavement.

"Do you know what the fuck we're going to have to do to get back?" said Summer Raine. "All my clothes."

"All my clothes and all my dope. Shit," said Luxury Dawn.

The men from Lady London's family watched through the windows to make sure they didn't come back. The women checked over their shoulders, wishing for Ruby and the Buick, but it seemed the entire city had been cleared out for bombs or disease. An ugly little city like all the rest they'd ever seen or lived in. Sun scraped and ragged brown and rotting inside just like poor Lady London.

"I even forgot how she died," Tammy said.

"How could you forget that?" Luxury Dawn asked her.

"I don't know. I've been so high. Wired every day. Even now."

"Hell, we all are," Summer Raine said. "Cranked the fuck

out to the gills."

"When did you forget?" Luxury Dawn said.

"If I knew that I could trace back when I knew to what I knew and bring it back to know it again now."

"Think about it for a while," Summer Raine told her.

"It'll come back to you."

"Do you think you ever remembered?" Summer Raine asked.

"I must have. But I can't get back there, you know?"

"Try to remember who told you," Luxury Dawn said.

"I'm trying, but there's nothing," Tammy said.

She couldn't even remember the names of these girls she was traveling with, but she knew their names were as pretty as homemade poems. She forced her own name from her mind and scuffed the bottoms of her sneakers on the cracked sidewalk to hear if her shoes might give her a new one. She listened hard for it. Storm clouds boiled into the sky above them and when thunder shook the dusty ground they jumped and held themselves and looked up to see what the sky would do next.

Honey Destinee Lavender Autumn Denver Cheyanne Wing Feather Delight Secret Wonder Dreamscape Twilight Mist Black Eye Rape and Strangle Tammy.

"I remember," Tammy said.

They were lined up on a bench inside a curbside bus stop shelter to hide from the rain that lashed the roof and streets with drops like glass marbles sent from a tombstone sky.

"Remember what?" Summer Raine said.

She had to raise her voice to speak over the storm. "How Lady London died."

They sat on either side of her and watched her talk.

"She drowned," Tammy said.

"She did," said Luxury Dawn.

"She got drunk and fell into the Arizona Project canal."

"I think some motherfucker pushed her in," Luxury Dawn said.

"Bullshit," Summer Raine told her.

63

"I think Pooh Bear held her head under," Luxury Dawn said.

"He'll hold your head under too," Summer Raine said.

"What was she drinking?" Tammy asked.

"She'd have drunk gasoline if you served her a glass," said Luxury Dawn.

"Twenty-four and alky dead. Alky drowned and alky dead."

"Twenty-four?" Tammy said. "Twenty-four?"

"How old you think she was?"

"Thirty or shit thirty-five."

And later, nothing left in their bloodstreams but screaming pollution. The shock of being left behind had passed a long time before and now they twitched and paced in a drenched and vicious and hopeless vagrancy.

"I know it was you who stole my dope last week," Luxury Dawn told Summer Raine.

"When have I ever stolen a goddamn thing from you in your whole life?"

"You were sad," said Luxury Dawn. "You were sad because you're not looking as good as you used to. Your Johns have been overlooking you, looking past you and looking through you."

"You go to hell."

"Why don't you check up in His Upper Room for His Upper Bone?"

"That isn't funny at all," Summer Raine said. "Making fun of Jesus."

Tammy walked along the curb to get distance from their rage. She might even walk back to His Upper Room now that the rain had stopped and the same men who had kicked them out would be waiting to pull her back inside to stick her in a casket once the rest of Lady London's family and the old fan-waving ladies all went home and Jesus had His Upper Room all to himself.

Luxury Dawn got into an Oldsmobile and with the driver smoked crack cocaine for three days and nights straight at a truck stop motel on the eastern edge of Tucson. When they ran out he sold his gold necklaces and watch and his gold bracelets and rings and when they ran out again he sold his Oldsmobile and at last tried to sell Luxury Dawn. And raving at him in the parking lot and swinging her purse, she attracted the attention of a truck driver named Buster who drove her to El Paso and San Antonio and Houston and New Orleans, where she escaped one night when Buster produced a hunting knife and tried to cut her throat.

Summer Raine hitchhiked for an hour before she gave up and sat on a schoolyard lunch table and waited for another storm to fall so that she might bathe off the sweat and dirt and so she might hold her mouth open to the sky to wash the scum out of her decaying mouth. But no rain came and she burned away her name and its smoke circled her face with the smell of name ash and her real name came back to her out of her empty veins. Cynthia Mack. And when she couldn't remember the last time anyone had called her that, she dragged the lunch table to a basketball hoop and climbed on top and hanged herself with her belt.

For a week Tammy lived with a family in their Monte Carlo at a rest stop just outside of Eloy. A mother and a father and their baby. They had needles and dope and the father kept a pet rat in a shoebox. He'd found it under a motel bathroom sink and his wife couldn't stand when he took it out of the box and fed it potato chips from his fingers. The rat took a pretty good chunk out of his knuckle.

"Shit," he said.

"Serves you right keeping a wild rodent."

"And what the hell serves me right keeping you?"

They'd all tied off and nodded as the storm drops knocked down on the roof. Between the rain and the depth of their dope sleep they didn't hear the baby screaming and didn't find her until the next morning. The mother's scream woke her and you could barely see the baby's face for how the rat had left her.

* * *

The nude juice bars stayed open all night long. No booze. Just soda and fruit juice and pussy juice and he watched out for ooze juice.

"But you better not pull on yourself. Even not through your pants. You pull on yourself through your pants and Feljah will give you the eighty-six."

A steel guitar from the speakers that didn't match the flashing or strobes or the girl laid out on the stage with her spread legs raised as if giving birth and rocking side to side for a handful of men who watched her twinkling sex as though it were a television.

"You been to nude juice before?" the man who took his money asked him and before he could answer he was already greeting another man and taking his money and calling, "Pussy, pussy, pussy," and inviting him to get a juice and sit with a friendly arm over his shoulder and his wet teeth glinting in rolling blue light.

He thought he saw a cross on the wall behind the stage. But it was only the girl's shadow with her arms out and her plastered smile stretched under the weight of her empty eyes. A warm smell in the greasy air. It had been there all along but now he was able to place it. A musk. A damp musk. Bitch heat. Then another girl. A black girl who disappeared behind a hissing cloud of fog then emerged teasing her inner thighs with her fingertips and at last the men clapped like lazy spanking. She was the one they had all come to see.

He didn't notice the men leave but for a while he was the only one left among the empty chairs. The country and the metal and the rap music that made him feel surrounded by winking menace in the shadows. He reached back and touched the lump of his wallet. You couldn't get a lap dance in a nude juice bar and he was glad none of the dancers came around to ask him if he wanted one. Animals scratching themselves and shitting in the sand.

Then some men in ties shambled in but didn't sit with one another. The girls recycled in rounds of three with their same sluggish enchantments of squatting and spreading with the same half smiles and soon none of the girls smiled at all.

Trouble from the changing room behind the stage. Cursing then a thud and then louder cursing. Two of the dancers staggered onstage and one had the other by the hair which fell a platinum animal held aloft in the dancer's fist. Naked lumbering of skinny glittered mannequins. The music quit and the bald bouncer Feljah pulled them apart and lifted the wigless girl and carried her away and the other one said, "Don't hurt her, don't hurt her," and a man in a tie clapped once and folded himself with a laughter so wild it looked like he was sobbing.

Weldon fell asleep and the first beats of a new song snapped him awake just as his head fell. A stage light and fog and red squad car strobe. A shopping mall haunted house doom and the drifting shadow of the cross on the wall behind her. Her song went *Foxy, foxy, foxy, your body's been on my mind.* He stood and called her name through his hands and knocked over chairs to the stage. He called her name so she'd get off her back.

"Tammy, stand up," he said and by the time he reached her she had. She squinted through the stage light and strobe. When she recognized her father she backed up and said something cruel he could only half hear and only with his eyes.

He climbed the stage and the spot died and the strobe died and what was left of the fog moved past him. He called her name and spotted three dancers watching from the side of the stage as Feljah wrapped his arms around him and lifted and carried him as he'd carried the girl offstage. His breath was a strobe and it shut off as well and when they reached the doors, he closed his eyes and braced himself for the pavement. But Feljah set him down and said, "You can't come back here. I know she's your daughter."

He tried to rush past but Feljah blocked him. "No," the bouncer told him. "No. You can't. I know she's your daughter but she's already gone. She's gone."

"Where?"

"I don't know, man. You have to go now."

"Hold it."

"No."

He didn't want to get back in the truck. He looked inside at the seats and they were as empty as answers. He waited for a merciful dancer to sneak out and tell him where she'd gone. But nobody came to tell him anything. The sign attached to the club read *Le Cabaret* and below that *Nude Girls 24 Hours*. It had nothing to offer his where. His truck had nothing to offer his where. Feljah had nothing to offer his where when he stepped outside with a flashlight and Weldon crouched behind the flatbed.

"I see you," Feljah called. "I told you to get the fuck out of here. And I'm not going to be so nice this time."

The stars a spray of bullet holes fired through a wall between tonight and tomorrow.

4

They rushed from the sunset under a cold wind of dust and the light itself a range of fires behind them rising into gradual embers that licked what was left of the sky over the desert that tumbled past a wreckage of rocks and dead scrub and the evil shifting shades of dusk and in her rearview mirror mountains spiked with fangs devoured the sun.

Then for a while the sky looked pretty and soft in its brush of purple sand until the last light leaked away and the night pressed down on every final color and the interstate speared straight into a pair of eyes. Six o'clock and seven o'clock narrow and mean on the edge of a lunge and a bite.

"Listen to this song," he said. He eased the volume up. Something country western sad. A whining fishing lure romance that set his face in a dull reverence behind his brown plastic glasses and his acne and his breathing. All that was missing out there in the sand were nuggets of cat shit black under the moon. Ahead of them a blue-red orb reaching into the sky and as they got closer, she saw it was a bright sign on a towering pole glowing the letters TA.

"Some dudes," he said. "Some dudes think that there means tits and ass. But it's Travel America. But even some dudes that know it's Travel America still call it tits and ass. Hey," he said. "Let's stop off and get us some candy and soda."

"Think we can get some booze?"

"I'm not old enough to buy alcohol. Besides, it's against my faith," he said and nodded once. "Assembly of God," he said. "I know I have a dirty mouth sometimes. I'll say shit and tits and sixty-nine. You know when two people—"

"I know what sixty-nine means."

She watched him eat down six Snickers bars in a row. The wrappers strewn on his lap and down by his feet. He sucked his fingers clean then guzzled down half a big bottle of Coke. He burped into his fist and downed the rest of the bottle and burped again and tossed it out the window. The on-ramp sign read I-10 East Phoenix and the only road the headlights caught was what seemed left of the world.

After two miles of silence he said, "When my granddaddy died they had a stereo set up at his funeral and played 'My Way' by Elvis Presley. Because that's how my granddaddy did things. He did things his way."

She saw the twitch in his lower lip and dreaded the sob that would follow.

"My granddaddy's name was Warren Sollars and that's how he did things. He did things his way."

Another hour and he held his stomach and his face soured and he told her he wanted to pull over at the next rest stop. He parked in an empty slot among a whole row of empty slots. He shut off the engine and the headlights and leaned his seat back and closed his eyes. She tried not to fall asleep but in the dark stillness she drifted. She was moving further and further from her worries and only seconds from passing through that soft wall when some wet noise he was making snapped her straight awake.

He was watching her while he pulled himself off. His jeans down over his knees and his bare lap white.

"Oh Jesus Christ," she said.

"You don't have to do anything," he said. "I just want you to watch me."

She covered her face. First her whole face and then her eyes and then her mouth with both hands like a child with a secret. His long blue car driving away and leaving her red in his taillights. She left the little walkway and passed a sign that said *Caution: Dangerous Wildlife* with a picture of a scorpion and a rattlesnake. She hadn't expected a chill this sharp in the desert any time of year. Christmas lights strung around the top of a toilet hut. Trucks lined up on the outer drive. She walked and stumbled on stones she couldn't see. Behind her the trucks looked like Christmas morning toys.

A parade of rattlesnakes and scorpions followed her in ordered rows like soldiers. They escorted her back down to the trucks and their diesel exhaust and the muted rumble of their resting engines like beasts growling in the dark warning you to stay away.

"I'll take you all the way to the end of the 'Star-Spangled Banner.'"

He crossed Cottonwood Springs Road and Box Canyon Road climbing between Hayfield and Cactus City and his engine started heating up so he pulled off at the Chiriaco Summit for water and radiator fluid. He bought some beef jerky and a bag of peanuts and topped off his tank even though he was only down a quarter. He was scrubbing his windshield when a boy who looked just eighteen scurried over and asked him in a desperate gasp if he had a cigarette.

"I hate to ask but some dude stole them and my cash off me in the toilet."

"I don't have cigarettes," he told him. "Don't smoke."

The boy was wearing a T-shirt with a surfing teddy bear on the front. It looked snug even on his hungry frame. His sneakers had a few holes and the ends of his jeans were tattered. He was queer. He surveyed the gas traffic with his hands on his little hips. "Man," he said.

Then he looked over and said, "My ride went ahead and

dumped me out here where Jesus lost his shoes. I would have drove but I honestly don't know a thing about driving a car. Shit."

"Where you headed?"

"The beach."

"What beach?"

"Guy who drove me wouldn't tell me. Just said the beach and the beach was enough for me."

"I'm sorry but I'm heading in the opposite direction."

"I didn't even ask you for a ride."

"But you were going to. And you probably still will."

"Not if you're not headed for the beach."

"I don't know about that. I imagine you'll get around to asking me anyhow."

He didn't ask him but in a production of high defeat climbed in as if this highway man and his truck had demanded it.

"Where you headed?" the boy asked.

"I told you. Opposite direction from the beach."

"What direction is that? I don't know these parts too good."

"East."

"Where east?"

"Not sure."

The talk dropped quicker than a brick off a bridge. The boy was frightened.

"I'm driving east until I find my daughter."

"Where is she?"

"If I knew that I'd be headed there directly."

"She in trouble?"

"A whole lot of trouble."

"What kind of trouble?"

"The kind of trouble girls get into when they run off without knowing where they're going or what they're going to do when they figure out where to end up."

The boy crossed his arms and for a while watched the desert pass out the window. By the smell of him he hadn't bathed in days.

"Tell me," he said to the boy. "Along with getting ditched and robbed, what kind of trouble are you in?"

"What makes you think I'm in trouble?"

"You smell like a dumpster and you're hustling a truck stop in the desert."

"Who says I'm hustling?"

"I say you're hustling."

"That's fine. Mind if I turn on the radio?"

"It's broke."

"How long's it been broke?"

"I don't know. Five years maybe."

"Here," the boy said.

He reached down and placed his hand over the radio and closed his eyes and murmured a long whisper of words and held up his other hand like he was taking an oath. He sat back and smiled and said, "Go ahead. Try it now."

He did. A blast of static like children screaming under a blanket. He lowered the volume and turned the dial and found horns and accordions on a Mexican station. He looked over at the boy and said, "How the hell did you do that?"

"Try to find some R and B."

"Tell me how you did that."

"I'm a magic faggot," he said. "If you're thinking about doing anything to me."

"Doing anything to you?"

"I'll give you stomach cancer."

The boy went quiet and shut the radio off and brought his knees up and wrapped his arms around them and rocked.

"I really wish you'd put your seat belt on," he told the boy.

"You a chicken hawk?"

"No, I'm not a chicken hawk."

"You're either lying or you aren't one. You even know what a chicken hawk is?"

"Yes, I know what a chicken hawk is."

"You kind of seem like you might be one."

"I'm not."

The boy put his legs down and buckled his seat belt and crossed his arms and looked out the window for a while. "I'm so fucked," he said.

"How so?"

"I'm positive."

"Positive about what?"

"I'm HIV positive."

When Weldon tried to turn the radio back on, nothing played. He twisted the dial to silence from the left to the end. The boy was shaking his head out the window at a desert as vast as a threat.

"Your folks know where you are?"

"What happened to your neck?"

"This whore stabbed me with a switchblade."

"Are you serious? What for?"

"She robbed me."

"Whores," the boy said. "Rats and roaches."

Late fall and the midday sun had lost its heat and its light behind a haze like a faded stain.

"My dad doesn't know where I am. He threw me out anyway. Caught me with a guy and locked us up and beat us both."

"Where you from?"

"New Mexico."

"Whereabouts?"

"Las Cruces."

"I got arrested there," Weldon told him. "Fifteen years ago."

"For what?"

"I was out of my mind shooting Methedrine a week straight with a crew of bikers out of El Paso. They ditched me at a rest stop. I finally went crazy and set the grass and the brush on fire in the median. Fire westbound and fire east. Spread so far they had to shut the interstate down a stretch."

"You still shoot speed?"

"No."

"I know where we can score some in Blythe."

He gave the boy a look and the boy turned to watch the razor teeth that reached from the top of the Mule Mountains. When he could tell the boy was still listening he said, "Did a year in Doña Ana County. My wife left and took our daughter to Oklahoma. I hadn't even asked her to bail me out. It was done. Then I drifted for a couple years. Trains. Trucks. Texas and Mexico. I'd get drunk on wine from a gas station and collect called the old number just to see if she might have changed her mind and moved back. I'd only really gotten a year of time with my daughter. I thought I was the biggest straight Satan who ever crawled out of the earth. I'm still trying to make up for it. But I won't. I know I won't. But sometimes I think I might be able to. Not make up for everything. But something. And if I can, then this is my last chance."

The boy was asleep, his head against the window. He slept as they crossed the Tex Wash and he slept when they passed Desert Station and he was still asleep when Weldon pulled into the Flying J stop just west of the California-Arizona line.

"This still a Greyhound stop?"

The man behind the counter said it was and Weldon asked for a ticket to Long Beach.

"Wish I could join you."

"Wish I could too."

The boy had bummed a cigarette and was standing by the pay phone out front and smoking. He looked even dirtier than when he'd picked him up and even skinnier. His face was white as a child's casket and his eyes and his cheeks were dark and deep. Like he was waiting for his last phone call before he let himself pass.

"Here," he told the boy.

"What's this?"

"Bus ticket to the Pacific Ocean."

He stuck fifty dollars into the boy's hand and said, "Get

yourself something besides a rail. A room and some food. You can't sleep on the beach this time of year."

The boy looked more frightened than thankful. "Can't talk," he said with a rasp that sounded even worse than the rest of him looked.

"I wouldn't have thrown you out," he told the boy. "I'm not saying I would have liked that kind of thing going on in my house. But I wouldn't have hurt you over it."

It wasn't until he crossed the Colorado River that he saw the drops of blood the boy had coughed up on the windshield. Some of it was smeared where the boy had tried to wipe it off.

Arizona State Line.

Arizona.

The Grand Canyon State Welcomes You.

When they did eat they lived on sweets from the bakery counter at the Basha's grocery a block down from the Crown Palms Motel. Chocolate doughnuts with colored sprinkles, glazed bear claws, cupcakes, butter cookies, wedges of vanilla pudding pies.

They carried it all back to the room under a howling roar of jets leaving the Phoenix Sky Harbor and closing down right above them as they landed. Tammy and Kayla watching them terror through the blue skies, sharp and shimmering monsters above them as they sucked the sugar goop off their fingertips.

They splayed themselves across the beds, a storm of grocery store bakery trash strewn about the room. Smeared tissue and cardboard and plastic. Flush with sugar and fat they tingled from their full bellies.

"Think we ought to make ourselves puke?" Kayla said.

"What the fuck for?"

"We might get fat."

"We'll be hungry in an hour. And then we'll have to cram ourselves with more shit. We won't need any help puking then."

"Still."

Kayla lumbered to the television and Tammy propped herself up on her elbows and watched her click around the dial until she stopped on a fuzzy channel discolored in flashes of green where a chubby preacher waved a leather Bible over his head and yelled down at his followers who sat rigid with the shame of their sins.

"Shit, Kayla. Let's watch something else."

"If you don't mind. I need to watch this for a while."

She blinked at Tammy a few times before she spoke again. "I know I'm a strung-out whore. But deep in my heart, I'm still a believer."

And when Tammy didn't understand, Kayla blinked again and said, "A Christian. I'm still a Christian."

And then she pointed at the television and said, "Besides. That man there," she said. "That preacher is my daddy."

"No that isn't," she said. "Your brain is cranked to fuck."

"My daddy, Tammy."

She brought her finger to her lips and raised the volume.

The preacher was between oaths and wiped a handkerchief across his brow. Two planks nailed together that formed a rugged cross on the wall behind him. A yellow phone number under the words *Prayer Line* appeared at the bottom of the screen and Kayla picked up the phone and pressed at the numbers until Tammy pulled the receiver out of her hand and slammed it down so hard the bell inside rang once.

"Goddamn you. We can't afford a long-distance call, Kayla. Damn motel will charge us double."

The preacher, Kayla's daddy, was speaking again. "I want to see the world the way my granddaddy seen it. But that's a world no more. And what way is that? The righteous way of our Lord and Savior Jesus Christ. The lily and white road to Paradise. The road that isn't stained with the filth of this world now. Cheating lying fornicating pornography."

He said nobody could ever get away from sin and pain and suffering no matter how good things were going and no matter how much love you poured into the world of your loved ones. Nobody. "I know a preacher who's a solid man with the Word in his heart and in his very mouth. And he raised his daughter with nothing but tender guidance and love. Love. Love of the Lord and the love of his own loving heart. But when his daughter turned eighteen, she up and left last year with her drugs and her liquor and her harlotry. A year ago and this poor man hasn't heard word one from her since. Not word one. Who knows where she is? Is she dead? She might even be dead. Dead in a ditch."

"I've got to get home," Kayla said. She paced the room, stepping through the bakery trash and packing up her things in the luggage of brown grocery bags she'd brought them in.

"Now wait a goddamned second," Tammy said. She shut the television off. "We had a deal. You know how much I'm going to have to hustle to cover this room myself?"

"I know. I know it. But you got to believe me that I'm sorry. I'm sorry," she said.

"Sorry? All you got is sorry?"

"I'm going to die out here, Tammy."

"And now I'm going to have to take it in the ass."

She watched Kayla scramble down the street out the doorway, another jet screeching overhead.

Six dates today.

Six dates tonight.

She slouched down the busy avenue and stuck her thumb out for an hour and finally got a date on his lunch break. He looked a lot like Kayla's preacher daddy and when she asked him if he was a preacher, he told her he didn't want to tell her what he was and he didn't have to. He pulled behind a motel court. "Milk it," he told her. "Goddamn you."

His face twisted and he filled the car with a groan that sounded like a deaf man auditioning for choir.

"Oh, God," he said through a wheeze. "I'm a goddamn middle school principal. There," he said. "And now you know."

She wiped her fingers on his seat and before she closed the

door, he looked up at her and sneered. "Hope you choke on it."

She slammed the door and kicked a dent in it before he gunned the engine and tore away, spraying her with pebbles and dust as she blocked her face with her hands.

Nothing for the next two hours. She put her thumb away. Then she extended it and held it out through the sunset and through the night. Six dates.

Six dates until she felt like all her teeth had been knocked out.

She didn't want to face the empty room as sick at herself as she was. And she wasn't too surprised when she found Kayla waiting on one of the beds. Her hair was sweaty and she was bouncing both legs on the floor. Tammy let the door shut and pretended she didn't notice her.

"Thought you went back home."

"My daddy wired me the cash but I never bought the ticket. I bought a load of crank and already smoked half of it. Now I have a sad tweak going on. But here," she said and handed Tammy forty bucks. "This ought to get us two more nights."

"I know how much it'll get us."

"I'll work tonight."

"You're goddamn right you will."

After Kayla left she got herself a six pack and knocked it down within the hour and cranked herself up out of Kayla's drift and left the room feeling like the Holy Queen of All Pimps to make sure Kayla was keeping her word. The sky where no jets at that hour dared to fly and a passing car honked. She coughed and felt a thirst but it was after one and her liquor store was closed and in her dry craving she forgot she was looking for Kayla at all. When she turned she saw how far she'd walked. Her feet already hurt straight through her arches and what was left of her drunk was getting cheap and low and dull. Like she'd just downed a whole bottle of mouthwash.

And here against some headlights the childish silhouette. Kayla's crouching shadow. She could tell her arms were crossed against her.

"How the hell you expect to get a date if you don't shake your little ass?"

When Kayla saw it was Tammy, she stopped. Her arms spread and then she turned to split in the other direction. Tammy only had to tell her once to stop. She did. Gave up and bent over with her hands on her knees. And even though she couldn't see her face, she knew the girl was pouting.

"You need to shake your ass," she said and stuck her thumb out to the empty street. "See?"

"There isn't anybody out here. How am I supposed to get a date now?"

"Show them your tits if you have to."

"Show who?"

"Show whoever the fuck drives by."

A little yellow hump of a car, scraped and pocked with rust, pulled up to the curb and Kayla raised her shirt and shook herself at it.

"If they don't stop, dumb hick. If they don't."

She waved the girl toward the yellow car and told her it was time to go to work. She saw a man in both seats.

Kayla said, "They want to know if they can pay both of us. Said they'd pay double."

"Pay us double or pay us both?"

She stuck her head back into the window.

"Pay us both."

"Get your figures right, Kayla."

The backseat was a box of their folded arms and legs crammed against the backs of the seats. The lights of the city and the lights above the streets fell away behind them.

"You can go ahead and pay us now," Tammy told them.

"My share," Kayla whispered.

"Later."

"Why not now?"

"Because I'm the bank. I roll the nickels."

The man in the passenger's seat said to the driver, "It's just like living in a pussy magazine."

The headlights shone on ugly open country then rose up a pass of rocky hills and clusters of prickly pear that grew so big you could count every needle. And then down the other side of the pass she felt the pavement leave off under the rolling crunch of gravel under the tires and she felt herself say, "Let us out now," the pound of her heart shaking her voice. "Here. Take your money."

"I don't want my money. I want to live in a real life pussy magazine."

Nothing but night on both sides. She fell offstage and out of the costume of her voice.

"You can have everything back," she said. "Please."

She felt Kayla put her face in her hands and shake her head. And weep.

"You can just let us out and we'll walk back."

The seats were pushed too far back to try to get to the doors. She was going to ask them what it was they wanted to do. What they were going to do. She told Kayla Quiet. The cash still in her hands. She told Kayla Quiet again and the man took his money back. She told Kayla Kayla Quit it and then the man shook up a little can with a red top, the kind mailmen carry for dogs, and a spray and a stream shot into their faces. Her face and Kayla's face. Kayla's face and her face. Right through their fingers. They writhed as much as they could in that space and they screamed. Their faces scalding. Their faces skinned and salted.

"Empty it."

And then they pulled them out.

They skidded across the gravel like tires. She could almost see and then she couldn't. He pulled Kayla away and the other one pulled Tammy. The doors still as wide as wings. And then she couldn't. Not even her own heels pulled across the rocks. Her head full of ants crawling through thousands of little holes. Her eyes squeezed shut and her throat clogged in on itself. He dropped her. She tried to crawl off and he yanked her back and his fist shut her whole face numb and the numb passed into pins and the pins into wrenches and hammers and the whole box they'd come from and she remembered how the nurse had said her name and when she opened her eye, she told her she had visitors. The nurse asked her if she wanted to visit with anyone and she nodded in her pillow and the nurse was gone and then she saw three girls in the doorway. Black curls full around their faces and the one of them had flowers and she thought there had been more but now she knew there were three of them. A bolt through her heart but by the sadness in their eyes she was sure they were not there to hurt her. They stood at the foot of her bed and told her they were sorry.

"We didn't think it would be this bad."

"These are for you. We didn't know if you had a vase so here's one."

"But if you already have one."

They closed their eyes and prayed and tapped their foreheads and chests and each shoulder with their fingertips and kissed the backs of their thumbs.

The next night on the floor reading through the taxis with her cigarette lighter she put the phone book away and saw the vase of their flowers and wondered how long they'd live after she left. Her father wouldn't remember to water them. But even if he did. Mexican flowers lived longer. Or there weren't any flowers anyway. Or the vase was just her reflection in the kitchen window.

She didn't want to see Kayla dead so she didn't move through the rocks and brush and cactus to find her. She moved down a path and then a road and the sun curled her over like an old bad lady. Her throat packed with splinters. Every breath the edge of choke. Wind like curling flames from ahead and from behind first on her cheeks and in her eyes and then on her neck and the backs of her ears. The end of that road to another road empty and black and hot. She put her thumb out. She put it down. She could only stick it out for so far and so high before a throb lit up in the middle of her shoulder and then she heard the harsh and distant whisper of her own name rasped from the bottom of an empty rock pit.

"Please don't leave me. Goddamn you, how could you leave me like that?"

She was holding her ripped and filthy shirt closed over her chest. Her face a squeezed fist tighter the closer she got. Then her face a red bulb around a pair of wild dirty eyes and yellow teeth clenched and set until she must have seen the shape Tammy was in and the rage drained and in Tammy's face she saw her own and in Kayla's face Tammy saw hers and they stared at each other through a wish that they hadn't survived the night and knew that they actually hadn't.

They walked until their shoes fell apart and they held them and eventually tossed them into the weeds. Dusk when they reached the city. They rested on bus stop benches and on pavement speckled with butts and broken bottle glass.

"Tammy, I need water. I need water bad. I don't feel good."

"As soon as we get back to the room. I promise."

"How long is that?"

"Twenty minutes maybe. An hour most. Maybe."

After another block Kayla stopped and lowered herself down onto the sidewalk.

"We have to keep going," Tammy told her. "Here, I'll help you."

But the girl wouldn't try to stand. Her shoulders sank and her back folded over and she laid on her back and jerked.

"Kayla. Kayla?"

Her eyes rolled up into her head and her body went spastic and a spastic sound jumped from her mouth in shocks. Tammy spun and screamed for help. No traffic to hear it. She shoved herself into a gas station and a clerk of mercy called 911.

Her seizure had quit and Tammy knelt and called her name and her flash of hope dropped when she saw that the girl's eyes captured nothing. The ambulance men took her away. They wouldn't let her ride with Kayla but a cop gave her a ride and she was glad he didn't ask her what had happened after he held the door for her to crouch into the backseat.

But he did say, "Your friend's probably going to die. You know that, don't you? That's the only reason I'm not hauling you in. You know better than to step off Van Buren. But that's the only reason I'm not hauling you in. Because your friend's probably going to die."

And she did. She died in the ambulance.

A nurse came out to tell her.

A nurse came out to tell her in the waiting room.

"And we know she was raped. Do you know when she was raped?"

"Last night."

"Do you know where she was raped?"

"Between her legs. Where the hell else you get raped?"

The nurse looked at her. "I'm sorry, dear. I'm sorry but Kayla's gone."

She'd known the girl for only two weeks. She'd find her preacher daddy on television and get to him through the prayer line. Maybe they could pray and that might be enough so she wouldn't have to tell him. Because she'd only known her two weeks anyway.

"Were you with her last night?"

"Yes."

"And he hurt you too."

"You know who did it?"

"Did he rape you too?"

Her bare feet slapped across the tile to the exit.

"Your feet are bleeding! Oh dear. Your feet."

Her key wouldn't work when she got back to the room. The skinny brown foreigner down at the desk told her he'd thrown her out. She hadn't paid.

"But I'm only like something what ten hours late."

"I'm not argue. I know you and I'm not argue."

"What you do with my stuff?"

"Go."

"Where's my shit, man?"

"Throw away."

"Where the fuck you throw away where?"

"I throw away. Away."

A haze of dust in the streetlights made a suck tube up and down both sides of the block. She looked back at the motel once and expected to see the foreigner standing at the office with his arms crossed waiting for her to return. But he was not there and she did not go back.

A pickup truck rumbled past dragging a clanging chain that scraped the street with a shower of sparks she could smell long after its taillights faded. She couldn't have faced the empty room straight anyway. The bag of Kayla's clothes was too dead to wear now forever. She stopped under the dust lights and the pain came back in waves that pulsed from the flame rods of her bones.

If I call your prayer line will you answer? Because if I had a prayer line coming to me and you called I'd pick it up. Even now this late at night.

I'll call you a cab to get here and tell you everything that happened.

He felt himself shrink around the depth of his empty stomach in the dark squeezing his steering wheel though the engine was off. Another rest area and he was starting to forget what she looked like. He could feel his arms but his head and his chest had been carved away. His watch was dead and so was the clock in the dashboard. He opened his eyes and looked east but saw no breath of light over the sharp ridge of mountains.

He went to the bathrooms and found a vending machine among them. He'd only vaguely emerged from his stupor of wasted fatigue, so when he saw the rat balancing itself on a ledge between two candy bars under the pale light behind the glass, he flinched and sucked in a fist of air.

The rat didn't notice. Peanut wrappers and peanuts themselves littered the top of the slot on the lid where the goods issued forth. Chocolate bars stood naked and brown over skirts of wrappers the rodent had torn open ragged. He nibbled nuts he held in his claws with rapid intensity, a beggar in the throes of starvation. He climbed from ledge to ledge, pulling himself up on coils that would otherwise push and drop whatever purchases were made.

But the rat dropped nothing. He embraced the bars of chocolate and coconut with a nimble balance on each edge, tearing with his long teeth and then chewing behind his jowls, his whiskers twitching and his little eyes sharp and alert. Once or twice he darted his head up to find what he might attack next.

The rat had just stripped the wrapping off a Baby Ruth when he froze, hunched forward, and brought his claws to his mouth as if to clean them. Compassion rose warm in Weldon's chest. He touched the glass with his fingertips and a dawn he didn't notice opened behind his back. The rat curled, twitched, then fell to the trap at the bottom with a clunk.

A man behind him whistled and when Weldon turned, he saw a squat shadow moving toward him with the hideous backdrop of a blue new day that promised nothing but sadness.

"What in the fuck happened to all that candy?"

The man stood before the machine, his hands on his hips or on the rolls that hung over his belt. He stared for a while before he finally shook his head.

"You try to steal all that candy with some kind of stick? With some kind of hanger for clothing?"

He looked over his shoulder, squinting.

"It was a rat," he said to the man.

"A rat?"

"Yes."

"Well shit. Where the hell did he go?"

"He's still in there."

"What?"

"Inside the machine."

"Kidding me."

"He died."

"Kidding me."

Weldon shrugged. His exhaustion had crossed into a new limit he'd never before known.

"How'd he die?"

"I think he ate too much candy."

The man shook his head and beheld the machine and its unbelievable mystery.

"I know some drivers who keep rats as pets. Right in their rigs. For company. Build them little hammocks that hang from the roof. They set there on their shoulders and the drivers feed them cheese."

He shook his head again at one confounding truth after another, the morning about them brightening. He looked over his shoulder and said, "So you think the chocolate did something to him?"

"I do."

"Where the hell in there is he?"

"He's down in the basket."

"The what?"

"The slot."

"Well let's see."

Bending forward squeezed his breath with a wheeze. He felt around, reaching as if for a prize. He screamed and yanked his hand out but the rat had already gripped skin in his teeth. He slapped at the rat and held his wrist and waved his arms before him. But the rat wouldn't let go. It looked like it had gained ten pounds since Weldon had first seen him fall. Nothing really dies if you wake it soon enough. A fist of electric cells pulses with energy for hours. From jewels that shimmer deep inside mountains without light and from rivers that run from sources deeper still.

He found himself sitting. The injured man was gone and the

rat had somehow gotten back into vending machine. Two drivers in cowboy shirts were rocking the machine on either side.

He couldn't tell whether they were trying to free the rat so they could kill it or to get all that candy to themselves or both.

5

They showed her the track that ran from the back of the weeds into the lots between the rows of rigs where the drivers slept. You stepped over a sheet of chain link folded over in the dirt pulled down from the rest of the fence to keep the whores out. But how you going to keep them out when the drivers are waving twenties out their windows? You're lucky. Last year they built up a mess of lights all over the lot. Up and down the track. Shining down on the weeds even. But the drivers complained they couldn't get no rest. It was bright. Bright. I don't give a fuck. Leave me alone. You got a cigarette? No and I don't give a fuck. You will. You'll give a fuck highway quick.

She slept in cars and in cab sleepers when she was too wasted to tell the drivers to stop it. Stop. Sometimes in a tent past the chain link in the weeds before the mesquite trees and all their branches and all their thorns and all their screech bugs sucking themselves wet out of their shells.

They showed her how to bathe with wipes. Broken bottles and garage bags and couches and tires and pink shirts covered in bug holes and bloody underwear and rubbers and flattened purses missing their straps and glass pipes crushed to dust.

She watched a ragged girl come back to have her baby on a couch in the weeds. The girl thought she might find the father. That the baby's screams would bring his daddy out of the showers and out of the diner and out of the video games and out of ten different trucks to pick them both up and drive them off into ten different directions. But something happened after the baby was born and nobody came to see if it might be his. Something happened when the baby lay squirming and squealing on the ripped towel she'd found. Something happened when she paced up and down the weeds calling Hey! Bloody and white and wet in the weeds. It was both morning and some kind of dusk. Bloody and white and wet in the weeds then lumbering out onto the track into the lot and talking to herself. Lurching. Full run. Right into the drive around the lot where a blue Lincoln was speeding through. No headlights. Skidding tire smoke and a swerve and a horn and it was both morning and some kind of dusk as her arms and legs twirled across the air.

Her baby turned into a fang rage baby and the church people came to take him away.

Sometimes the church people brought them gallons of water out of the back of a church station wagon. Sometimes the men from the same church would come back at night. Alone in the church station wagon or in their own little cars. You always knew it was them with their brown plastic glasses and greasy belly fat.

She slid in and out of sleepers and cars and rooms and vans and tents and toilets and once or twice the race car video game between the gift shop and the showers. And once in the back of the television lounge and the thin smoke above the seats.

She'd tried to keep track of the days in the dirt. She was only going to be out there a month. One month on the track that ran from the back of the weeds. A stick in the dirt for the date. A mesquite stick with a thorn she couldn't break. Then she lost five dots worth of days in a storm and she wondered how many days she'd been at the track and she wondered how many days she had left. Not only on the track but in the rest of her life because keeping track of one was just as important as keeping track of the other. Now she'd have to keep track in her mind because you never knew when a storm would wash the keeping away. In her mind. Her mind. Last thing she'd think about before she crashed and the first thing she'd say to herself as soon as they woke her up no matter where they woke her up. But then she'd stagger around for an hour before she remembered she'd already forgotten.

"What's wrong?"

"Nothing. I forgot something."

"What did you forget."

"Nothing."

"Come here and remember this."

She tried to keep track of the days in the stars as they lined with the moon but they looked the same every night. You'd have to sleep in exactly the same place every night for it to work. You lost them like sand washed off in a creek. You lost them like you lost a way out you were sure you had. You lost them like the hours you spent walking the tracks between trucks. When they spit on you. When they pitched jugs of piss out their windows. Where could you go? What would you tell anyone about where you'd been and what you'd done? Then they kick you out of the toilets for good and you hold your nose and squat and drop your mess where everybody else does.

In the wind she touched her head to make sure she still had her hair. A wind so fierce and so wild she was sure it had moved all the stars to the sky over the other side of the world.

She'd wonder where that baby was now. She asked another girl where the church people and the cops took the babies once they got them.

"Shit if I know and shit if I care. Baby jail. Who the hell knows? Don't talk about babies out here."

Deeper down a dumpster filled with rats. She'd long since lost the bounce in her flesh and when she sat on the dirt with her legs crossed she could feel her ass bones stabbing through. Rat lung fuzzy and rat lung dry. Every cough scraping up her throat with a knife in a fist of bones. Grains at the bottom of the glass. Burn and crackle and smoke. Blue smoke and glass smoke and black smoke burning. Freebase rock cocaine and Arizona desert crank out of glass tubes a pimp called Roo Roo Regular overcharged the girls twice what he paid at Starlight Liquor.

"You think you're working alone out here but you aren't," a green toothless whore asked her one night as she was walking back to the weeds.

"I know I'm not."

"How old are you?"

"That's my business."

"Come on. Don't make me fuck you up."

"Eighteen."

"Eighteen? Then I feel sorry for you."

"Well I wasn't asking for nobody's pity."

"And I didn't ask you whether or not I could give it."

"How old are you?"

"Thirty. But I only been out here a year and a half. Let me tell you something, girl. Remember, this is where you end up when the rest of the world is done fucking you. When you're too wasted and you stink too bad to suck anybody's dick. You? Eighteen? You still have time for both. Years. Eighteen. But you got to get off this track. Now. You're strung the fuck out. Lost all your skin. Lost all your color. Hair's falling out. Open your mouth. Let me see your teeth. Come on. Let me see. Getting meth rot too. I don't want to smell your breath. Jesus. Jesus. Get off the track. Get off the track and get off the track now."

Mostly white girls but some black girls and some Mexican girls too and even a few Indians. You paid one of the pimps for your space on the track and as long as you kept paying, they left you alone.

One night some truckers chased this little white pimp back into the weeds and beat him to death with axe handles. He'd tried to rob one of them in his sleeper. None of the girls would ever pay him. They'd laugh. He called himself Magic Ghost and he'd only been there for two weeks. He told everybody, "I'm the brand-new thing." Then he'd walked around the weeds and the track like he was looking out for prospects, rubbing his hands together and singing, "Meat hook pussy. Pussy, pussy, pussy. Nasty old pussy."

They shined their flashlights around for a while and then carried him out in a black body bag.

"Shit, I seen him!" said a black whore run out of her own mind by how many sweat and piss reeking years the track had yanked out of her spirit.

"Bullshit, Shondra."

"His brains were a bowl of bloody oatmeal in those weeds."

They rolled their eyes and went back to work.

"It doesn't matter if you call him Jesus, Mohammed, or Glory to God!" she called after them. "He isn't here. He isn't here. Is he here? No, he isn't here."

But they all seemed to believe Shondra anyway, since nobody went anywhere near where the dead little white pimp's brains had spilled. A spot in the dirt under a mesquite tree. A tree that was set aside from the rest. But not too far. Because she saw. Because she came to see.

"Where the fuck Baby Child going?"

To find a way. To find a way to tell Shondra she was right. To find a way to tell Shondra about the way the dirt looked and what she would find in it under that glaring hour. There under the branches of thorns she picked at the black dirt and drew what she knew in her blood was the date. Then she dug in the black dirt when she felt the portal that swallowed the date and his brains and his last thoughts rushed down into the portal and water burped out of the portal and smoke and when she waved it away she saw that the date had returned and she stood and stared at the black dirt under her nails and the skids across her knuckles.

"What the fuck you doing back there? Get out."

She hit the track. Her hands before her. Her black dirt of brain hell hands. Two drivers saw her. One of them shook his head.

"That's a whole lot of lizard right there."

"Puts the lizard in a whole lot of lot."

Then she was back in the weeds even though she didn't remember walking back. Her shoes were missing and she didn't bother looking for them. The bottoms of her feet were black too. She felt the black spreading. She felt the rest of them watching it spread.

"You been here two months are you're already dying," a man standing above her said. "I hear you're only eighteen, Baby Child."

She looked up at him for a while. She tried to stand but could not. When she tried to speak, she could only cough.

"Are you? Are you eighteen?"

She nodded.

"I can help you. I can get you out of the weeds and off the track for clear and for good."

She'd seen him around. His long hair and the frost on the tips of his spikes.

"You want a real bath instead of wiping yourself down with wet naps? You want regular meals and a regular bed? Then follow me," he said. "Come on. Follow me."

He walked the edge of the lot along the rows of slumbering semis and under the floods where moths circled like souls battering the ceilings of a hell's burning cave. The longer he walked the fewer the lights and soon the monstrous engines rumbled in the dark. And then the rumbling at his back he caught the Party Row fuck reek smog thick in his nose and a girl in a skirt scampered past and smelled of what it was he wasn't looking for and darted back the way she came, which was into the dark all along the edge of the lot. A dark he faced walking through his own slouch. Red cigarette ends and lighter flames sparking to life the peeking night eyes of animals and insects watching through the thicket. Then a rough laugh and a cough and a woman's voice raspy and low and adamant. "Ten, ten dollars," the voice said.

He stuck his hands in his pockets and found that his pockets had somehow gotten deeper. Women emerged to watch him. They'd quit trying to look alluring in their dirty skirts and Spandex shorts and their legs had lost their shape away to smeared and wrinkled poles with rough black knees and their faces were pocked like abandoned roads. The dead arisen from anonymous Jane Doe graves. They'd fallen right from home and straight into these trucks and these weeds. They'd never even had a chance to tumble out of topless bars.

A man's voice. Young and white and trying to sound black. "Buy or bye-bye," he called, but he couldn't see the face the words had come from.

Within minutes he quit trying to hide his money. "I need to find her," he said. "She's gone. She wasn't even here to begin with."

"You're in the wrong weeds."

"Cowboy cracker. Get back on your horse and ride the fuck gone. Gone."

"Your daughter wouldn't be out here if you hadn't fingerfucked her."

A lanky white pimp with bad teeth and a ball cap on backwards and holding a heavy black girl by the arm. "This is my lizard," he said, moving her arm like he was trying to wake her up. But she wouldn't. She didn't smile or blink or frown and looked right past Weldon to the rest of the empty desert into which she wanted to escape. "My black ass lizard. Go on," he told her. "Turn around and show him what that ass is made of."

When she didn't turn he turned her himself and spanked her a few times until she jiggled in her ballet tights with nothing on underneath.

"Like two pigs fighting in a wheat sack."

"I'm not looking for pigs or ass or wheat sacks, man."

"Crank, toot, smack, angel dust," the pimp counted off the ends of his fingers.

"My daughter."

"Let her be where she went."

He took the girl by her arm and guided her back. "If she split on you it means she must not dig your company no more."

"How much is it worth to you?"

He let the girl go and she walked off into the night.

"How much you willing to pay?"

"I'm not buying your junk or your piece of pussy. Just tell me how much."

"My wisdom's worth fifty."

"Here," he said. "Now goddamn tell me."

"You almost just missed her. She drove off yesterday."

"She has a car?"

"Roo Roo drove off with her."

"Who?"

"Roo Roo Regular. A pimp. Roo Roo Regular."

"He black?"

"He's white. Heavy metal white. Know what I mean?"

"Drove her where?"

"Phoenix."

"How do you know that?"

"Because that's the only place Roo Roo Regular knows where to go. He's never been anywhere else. Not even California. Not even Utah. And he's Mormon. Or at least he used to be. Real name's Rulon. That's where Roo Roo comes from. Listen," he said. "Your fifty's running a little low. In fact, it's about running on fumes."

"Here," he said, and shoved a twenty at him. "Where do I find him?"

"Just ask. Ask up and down Van Buren."

"Who? Ask who?"

"Anyone, baby. Everyone knows him. Everyone. They might as well call Phoenix Roo Roo Regular Arizona."

Two meals and one tank of gas away from nothing. He couldn't remember the last time he ate. He didn't know what it was called but he'd never seen so small a restaurant in his life. He had never heard country playing so loud through a floating blue wall of cigarette smoke. Nobody was eating anything. And then he knew he wouldn't be eating anything either. And when he looked back at the door he decided not to leave. One empty stool left.

Wet smiling eyes on either side. He couldn't hear what they were saying but he nodded anyway and then instead said something to them:

"I haven't had a drink in fifteen years," he announced over the music.

The last one had been vodka and this first one would be vodka and this time there would be no last time. No last anything.

These were all special effects in a movie of moisture running down his brow. Everyone in interstate costumes. Stetsons and Justin boots and Wranglers and checkered shirts with spunk-colored snap studs all up and down the front and silver belt buckles bigger than the faces of the costumed fools who wore them. The steel guitars shitkicker whining and the fiddles a screech of tears. The strangers on either side of him left and new strangers took their places and they nodded at him and at the bartender and sucked at their bottles in silence. Their own silence under the music and what wild hilarity issued from the tables and booths behind them.

He wavered and stopped himself before the bartender noticed. The stools on either side were empty and nobody came around to take them. Nobody he sensed wanted to take them. But the rest of the place was still packed. The bartender before him running his finger across his throat.

"Done," he said.

"Done."

"I'm cutting you off."

When his face fell back into his hands, he knew he had been for some time and was still weeping over half a glass of vodka that was gone by the time he opened his eyes.

"I paid for that."

He held himself up against a phone pole and when he tried to get back in, the doors were locked and the windows dark.

His headlights swerved over the little Pima Reservation roads he'd taken to avoid the highway police. The line of yellow lights of the city in the distance. He awoke skidding along the dirt at the edge of a drainage ditch and pulled over and slapped both sides of his face. A brown mutt trotted past, her belly of tits swinging underneath. Every dog, even the bitches, would forever be King in resurrection. He clamored out of the truck and yelled, "Hey!" Middle of the pocked and colorless road. She trotted away, but when he called to her again she halted and watched him. He clucked his tongue and held out his hand and again she ran off. He chased her for a few yards before he ran out of breath.

It wasn't that his truck had disappeared. It was that he had disappeared from his truck because the rest of his gas had disappeared and almost all of his money and the gas station burrito had disappeared and fifteen straight years had disappeared and King had disappeared and King's bitch had disappeared. Phoenix had not disappeared. He could see right there its bright yellow horizon. Tammy had not disappeared. Roo Roo Regular had not disappeared.

"I think his real name is Rulon Real," he said.

He threw up his arms and let them drop over his head.

He tried to spend his last few dollars on a bottle of wine out of a gas station icebox but it was locked and when he asked the clerk to open it, the clerk told him it was too late.

"Don't think I would have sold to you anyway. How many folks you beg for that?"

"No! I gave it begging. I gave it away begging. This all I got left. This is it."

"This isn't a soup kitchen."

A few of the motels he remembered on Van Buren had shut down. They were still standing but boarded. He was still standing but boarded. Already the sun seared him from the sidewalk as well as the sky.

He hadn't known King was still following but he was waiting for him when he came out of the Circle K with a cold bottle of Night Train in a paper bag. She was not King's bitch. He was King. King! He scouted a place to hide with his wine. But then he wasn't King. He was a man with no shoes demanding a dollar for a cup of coffee in a big city accent from back east.

"Come on, a cup of coffee."

"I'll bury you again!"

The bag disappeared right out of his hands and so had the bottle and after one block walked and one corner turned so was the barefooted man who'd taken it.

The bus driver spotted her sneaking a drink out of her purse and kicked her off and she walked up the aisle past a couple whistles for her legs.

It was too hot to walk with her heels over her shoulder but there was a liquor store on every corner and she'd been lit since yesterday and now she'd have enough to stay drunk all month. He'd paid for the room two weeks in advance and it hadn't taken long to find his roll of twenties in the glove box.

She could almost stand getting stared at. Eyes over lowered shades and eyes squinting over steering wheels and from behind liquor store registers.

The only man who hadn't stared bumped into her. He was walking down the sidewalk with his eyes closed, muttering and skinny as cancer behind a muff of beard.

"Watch your ass," she told him.

"Oh sorry," he said without facing her. "Sorry, sorry, sorry."

He found the barefooted wine thief in the shade behind the public toilets in a park of sun leathered transients napping on their piles of black garbage bags. The thief's legs were crossed and his back against the wall of concrete blocks. He looked up mid sip from the twist of brown paper wrinkled around the mouth.

"I want my damn wine back."

The thief shrugged. "Here."

Half a swig left at the bottom. He held it to the sun and sloshed what was left against the green glass. He glared at the thief and lifted the bottle and drank.

"You don't need no wine, man. You're about to die standing straight."

"I'm looking for someone."

"For ten bucks I'll tell you whether or not I've found him."

"You already got my wine."

"Most of it. Besides," he said. "That was no bottle of ten-dollar wine. But shit, fine. Who?"

"Roo Roo Regular."

"Wow, Roo Roo Regular. Well I'm sorry to say I'm sorry."

"Sorry."

"Roo Roo Regular got stabbed over in the Deuce last night. In the Deuce! Bar called Hanky's. You know Hanky's? Right next to that topless theater. He got stabbed in the throat in the Deuce and he bled all over Hanky's floor to death."

"To death."

"To death. Roo Roo Regular is Dead Regular. Roo Roo Regular is Throat Stabbed to Death Regular. Shit. Pitch that fucking bottle before the pigs bust us for public."

He tried to get sick but nothing came up. Just a strangling dry wretch from his gut up to this throat. The water in the sink only stayed on for a few seconds and he couldn't cup his hands together in time to get a drink. If there had been a mirror he would have tried to find her in it, behind him and in his eyes and in the way his voice said her name and then his own.

"The sink, man. The sink. Space, space, space."

It was not the wine thief but a one-legged yellow skeleton on crutches with his empty pant rolled up and tied off at the stump with duct tape. He watched the man orchestrate a series of rapid and efficient gestures that allowed him to keep the water on and drink from his hands at the same time. He leaned over and splashed his face, rubbed water across the back of his neck, up both arms, never once leaving his crutches.

He filled his mouth one last time and spat and told Weldon, "If you need a meal, you go to Saint Mary's parish on Second. Stay away from that Living Waters Mission. This is the only water living around here. Only thing is, they lock this place up at nine. Otherwise all the faggots in here start giving each other blow jobs. Have ye a cigarette, brother?"

He shook his head.

"Oh well then. Stay away from that Living Waters Mission. They'll make you listen to three hours of Bible before they give you any grub. Not a bite. You need a meal? Go to Saint Mary's Parish on Second. And if you need smokes, you better fly a sign. Seventh Street off-ramp. Lucky seven, man. Lucky seven."

The nails in his stomach. "I'm not homeless," he said to the man as he hobbled out.

The stark shine off the glass buildings and the red hills at the end of the boulevard where more glass, the glass of passing traffic and the flash of their fenders passed on waves that shattered like the vicious laughter of thousands. You bow and rise under this Pentecost when you wonder if you'd ever really wanted to find her in the first place. Your tongue a pink rock stuck in your mouth and your mouth the hot bottom of the avenue you walk.

If he got to the red rock distance it would be too late, the glass buildings already shrinking behind him.

Mexican boys with no shirts riding silver bicycles all twinkle and tire and chain.

"You see my Tammy?"

"No, man. You see mine?"

He tried to head back downtown but the shining glass blinded him. Brown smog sinking over the rest of the mountains hot as old black Africa.

"You see my Tammy?"

They'd all lost their voices on the sidewalks at bus stops and at the soda machines out front of the Dollar General with greasy babies in their rank diapers. At the bus stops getting on and at the bus stops getting off.

"You see my Tammy?"

He held his hands over the nest of nails the invisible wicked crows had finally finished building. He held himself and bowed and then straightened. Here the streets were vacant and the little houses sat dying on either side. And down the block a steeple topped with a golden cross and the sign out front said *St. Mary's Roman Catholic Church. Sunday Mass 8:00 10:30 12:00 1:30 Spanish* and lastly below everything else *Perpetual Adoration.*

He didn't need a meal, and he wouldn't have been able to eat a plate of steak if you stuck it under his face. He needed water and shade. Water more than shade. He didn't know how many steps in him he had left. He didn't think the church would be open but it was and a wall of cool dark held him in the doorway. And then the whole marble bowl of water he scooped into his hands and drank. He sat in an empty bench. All the benches were empty. All of the church was empty with the red glowing rows of little candles in glasses at the feet of sad statues in robes on either side of the church. Jesus Christ bloody terror with his arms stretched out and nailed to the wood.

He stood and went back to the marble bowl for more water and found that he'd already sucked it dry. He knew at once that he would never find her and that he'd long since given up trying. And then he knew he'd never tried as hard as he could have and that he'd long since given up trying at all.

"I'm not homeless," he told the agonized Christ.

They found him in the shade of a billboard later that afternoon. A billboard in Spanish for Mexican beer. First the kids with their ball on their way to play soccer in the same lot where he lay. It was one hundred fifteen degrees and his organs were shutting down. They'd thought he was just another bum until they saw the stitching in his tan leather boots. They were dusty but the stitching was something and so was the leather and so were the shape of his heels. And then the ambulance. They woke him up and turned him over onto his back and asked him questions he couldn't answer. He couldn't open his eyes either. But he knew they were from an ambulance. And when they got him inside and sped off they told him he'd be fine. He just needed some fluids and rest.

"I didn't try," he said.

"What didn't you try?"

"I didn't try to find her."

"Your wife? Your girlfriend?"

"My daughter."

"Mister, is she here in Phoenix? Is she someone we might be able to call? Do you have any other loved ones here we might be able to reach? Do you have their number?"

6

She'd wandered sick and sweating through hours of night until she found herself in front of the same hospital where they'd taken Kayla to die. The red letters above her said *Emergency* and the light fell over her like taillights. Pain through her bones and her muscles were bound with white hot wires. Her veins went dry and filled with dust.

"I need help," she told the woman at the desk.

"With what?"

"With what the hell you think?"

"You don't need to raise your voice."

"Please. I'm sick and I need help."

"Where are you sick and what are you sick with?"

"My whole body. Everywhere. Please."

"And what are you sick with?"

"Drugs," she said. "I'm sick on drugs."

"What drugs?"

"Crank."

"Methamphetamine?"

"Yes."

"Do you inject it, smoke it, or snort it?"

"Only thing I haven't done is eat it."

The woman gave her a look.

"Anything else?"

"Rock cocaine. Freebase. I'm sick."

"I understand."

"Booze. Alcohol," she said. "I got alcohol poisoning."

"I doubt that. If you had alcohol poisoning, you wouldn't be standing here and talking to me."

"I know I'm sick with something is all."

"When was the last time you used methamphetamine?"

"Two days maybe."

"Take a seat."

"How long's it going to be?"

"About two hours."

"But there isn't nobody here."

"There will be."

"I'm the first one in line."

"You're not shot or bleeding and any minute will come a whole load who are."

And there were. In line behind her and soon filling the seats around her where she sat. Nothing changed outside of this brown hell. Her feet felt like they were crying. A man told his weeping wife, "Sit. Sit or I'll sit on you."

Toddlers whined and behind her an old man groaned while he squeezed his head between his hands and she felt like she was crammed inside a broken music box of wailing lullabies on the skids at the bottom of a closet stuffed with ruined toys. Then her own shaking pain mounted and almost drowned everything else out.

She went to the desk to see how long it was going to be. "Two hours."

And she went back to the desk so many times the woman quit answering or even looking at her.

"Next," she said.

The room so packed that the newly arrived sick had to hold themselves up against the walls. And there hung the classroom clock. One in the morning on a Friday night and the sick assembled as the students and the intake desk lady the teacher and she

105

the student teacher's aide and for homework now you've all fucked your lives or you were already born good and fucked and you putter around the streets on your booze fume engines until they break down and you have to suck your way back to wherever you came from.

Sweat tickled the top of her scalp with the menace of spiders. When it ran down her forehead she wiped a drop away and got a whiff of the back of her hand and choked on the reek of spoiled meat and something like burned hair she'd never smelled before.

"Can't you smell it?" she asked the desk lady.

It was all the speed leaking out. She felt it drain out the back of her nose and down her throat.

Please rise for the Pledge of Piss.

"Thorazine," the doctor told her.

She awoke in what she would learn was called the day room. She was in a blue paper shirt and pants and she was sitting on a firm couch next to a bug-eyed girl roughly her age who was watching the television on the wall above them. The air conditioning was a pair of blue hands at the end of a kind and frosty God.

The girl turned to her in a sudden animation with her hands balled up under her chin as though Tammy had just shared a tender commitment of love.

"Do you know today is Bright Tuesday by the calendar of the Byzantine Eastern Rite Catholic Church?"

"No, I didn't know."

The words crawled out of her mouth, which then hung open under her hanging lids and the hanging thoughts napping in her hanging mind.

In his little office her social worker told her she'd been in the hospital five days.

"You came in as high as a meth skyscraper. A condemned skyscraper getting leveled down to dust by a demolition crew. Boom! Is that where you want to be, do you think?"

"Today's Bright Tuesday."

"That's fine. You want to be a garbage can your whole life?

Folks will stick anything they want into a garbage can. Men folks especially. You know that by now. You'll even fold yourself up and stick yourself in yourself and gobble yourself down to nothing left. You understand what I'm saying to you?"

Her brain was packed with cotton and her slippers shuffled down the hallway tile as she worried her fingertips and stopped to watch the other women with their crayons and coloring books. A woman in glasses with a gray bun shrugged and smiled and said, "You get burned out on television."

But the Bright Tuesday girl had not gotten burned out on television. She saw Tammy and waved her over and patted the empty cushion beside her.

"Listen," she said, leaning in like she was on the edge of sharing dangerous gossip. "Today is the Feast Day of the Glorious Saints Cyril and Methodius according to the calendar of the Byzantine Eastern Rite Catholic Church."

"Oh."

"Yes!"

"Hey," she said. "How long they keep you here?"

"Now that depends."

"Depends on what?"

"Depends on if you're adult psychiatric or adult detox and rehab. Are you adult psychiatric or adult detox and rehab?"

"I don't know."

"You must find out! If you find out then you'll know how long they're going to keep you. Oh," she said. She looked over both of her shoulders, squinted, moved in closer and said, "Can I ask you something?"

"Sure."

"Do you know what giving head means?"

"It means sucking a dude's cock."

"I wish you wouldn't talk that way. It's foul."

"You're the one that asked."

"A woman asked me at breakfast if I gave my husband head. I didn't know what she meant and when I asked her everyone at the table laughed. They can be so mean here! Has anyone here been mean to you?"

"No."

"Just watch out. This can be a place of true cruelty. Some of these women are bad old witches, okay?"

Her social worker told her she was first admitted as adult detox and rehab.

"And you still are. But then you'll be registered as adult psychiatric."

"Why?"

"At intake you expressed suicidal ideation followed by what you communicated as an actual plan to hurt yourself. To end your life, more specifically."

"I what?"

"You told the intake coordinator that you had all sorts of ways you wanted to die. You said you wouldn't mind throwing yourself under a train in the desert. You said you wished a gang of truckers would beat your brains in with axe handles in the dirt in the weeds in the track."

"How long do I have to stay here?"

"Depends on how much longer you want to stay the way you were."

"I don't want to stay that way anymore. Look. I'm not crazy."

"Nobody said you were."

"And I'm off drugs."

"You've been off drugs for a week. One week. A start, but nowhere near a monumental barometer of change. You checked yourself in. Said you needed help. And that's what we're here to give you. Help."

They came and went but he couldn't understand what any of them said. He knew they were telling him how he'd ended up there and what was wrong but they were too quiet. Quiet under the cold air and their misty whispers. They'd opened the windows and it was winter in Wyoming in Cheyenne, the best place in the world to drink yourself to death while you got pelted with dry burning snow.

They gave him a button at the end of a cord to press for help and he fingered it like a gift gem he would never wear. There was a white winter bird behind his head that burped a low chirp every five seconds. They wouldn't let him sleep. They kept checking him. They called him every time his eyes closed. The bird was trapped way the hell up here in Wyoming.

But one night they finally cut the lights and told him he should get some sleep and put a needle full of dope in his hand and told him to relax. It could have been morning but he couldn't tell and he didn't care and he knew the bird behind him had closed his eyes as well.

He could hear the frost on the window melt and run down the glass until the air turned cold and the glass frosted over again and the outside light shone through the ice and cast a sparkle across the walls.

"Tell me why you left us."

"It's a long, awful story you're not ready to hear and I'm not ready to tell."

"I wouldn't have asked you to tell me if I wasn't ready."

"Someday I'll tell you."

"We don't have a someday. You might leave me again before you have a chance to tell it."

"I won't."

"You did before. Why?"

"Tammy."

"Why?"

"All right. You reach an age when what you thought you needed turns into something else. What I mean is you reach an age when you need something else instead. And what mattered before doesn't matter at all anymore. You try to want it back all over again for some time. You reach back for it as far as your arms will go. Reach, reach, reach. Then you get tired and you quit reaching. Then you float along with nothing else left to care for. Nothing behind you, nothing in front of you, nothing sitting right at your side. And then something new comes along and you forget you had any life at all before whatever it is that finds you."

"I don't understand."

"You will once you reach that certain age."

"But I don't want to wait to know it."

"I don't know how else to say it."

"Try."

"All right. Part of it was all those distances I had to drive. All that time. Weeks. A month. Two months. And your faces went hazy on me. And so did my own face. There were other things that hazed you both away besides time. Besides all that distance."

"What things?"

"I guess all the things I gathered up to help me forget I was driving anywhere at all. And you know what sorts of things I'm talking about. The kinds of people who give you the kinds of poisons you take when you don't want to see back then or later on. And back then were your faces that had lost their shapes and the ways you both looked at me."

"You're making it sound like we left you."

"My shame cuts me open every second."

"You think that hurts worse than getting left by your daddy? You haven't told me anything."

"I just did."

"No, you didn't."

"I don't know what else to say."

Daddy, your face never went hazy on me. Mama never put your picture up but I could still see you. I put up my own pictures of you on every wall, inside and out. Every day. I drew you in school, and when the teachers asked who you were I just told them I didn't know. I remembered, as young as I was when you left. Don't you know I waited for you? I waited and waited, but you never came. You couldn't even find me, and I'm not even sure you wanted to.

They wheeled a sick old man out of the room under a sheet as white as Wyoming December and a while later a new sick man replaced him. Weldon watched him until a nurse pulled a curtain between them.

"Act one," the sick man said. "Intermission."

"How long I been here? How long I have to stay?"

The sick old man's son and the son's wife and the sick old man's grandchildren came to visit. They looked down at Weldon with pitiful fright as they passed his bed.

"What's wrong with that man?" one of the children asked.

"Quiet," his mother told him.

You might be right down there on the sidewalks. I could tell this to the electric heart bird and he could swoop on down through the Wyoming winter glass and tell you how I turned rotten as a pound of bacon and into a shiftless boy behind his wheel who quit caring about you. Who didn't want either of you waiting when I got back. That's the truth. My entire truth. But that bird is just a box of wires that can only tell me the sound of my own pulse. I can only tell this to myself unless I get out of here in time to tell it to you straight out of my strength. I don't think I've filed down the end of my second chance yet. I can still save you from the sidewalk because I'm still strong under all this sick. I can build you a whole new highway to get you across whatever it is that's trying to stop you. Because I think you've already gone ahead and reached that same certain age. The place where what you wanted back then is gone. I'll build you Interstate Tammy. Straight through. No storms, dust, or thunder. No traffic. A straight shot to the beach and an even straighter shot back home.

He tried to get up and the bird behind him bleated screaming torture. The family on the other side of the curtain was gone and so was the sick old man they'd come to visit. The curtain was drawn to the rest of the dark naked room. He didn't want

111

anyone to know he was leaving. The bird had him. A needle in his hand and some blood in the plastic.

A wind rushed him from under the bed. The bird was silent but the wind kept pounding in warm waves and then cold waves.

He felt for the call button but there was no call button to press. It had long since fallen and hung off the bed like a naked dangling suicide.

Her only preoccupation about the immediate future was lunch. She'd pad over to the menu posted on the dayroom wall with tape next to the television and knead her knuckles and piece every letter together until they yawned and stretched and settled into her hunger.

"Can't see!"

"Trying to watch the boob tube!"

"Oh, oh!"

They posted the menu for dinner exactly three hours after she'd finished lunch and the menu for breakfast an hour before bed. She was always hungry.

Her past was a different matter, no matter how much lithium and Thorazine they have her to keep it tucked away in the cotton and the fog. There was no place from which a woman could hang herself. Safely railings were flush against the hallway walls and in the showers and by the toilet. The edges of doors and nightstands and tables were rounded and smooth. The sheets were so thin they'd rip and fall apart if you tried. The past she hadn't actually seen was the worst: when, she wondered, had her father quit looking for her? Hadn't she told him she wasn't worth finding anyway?

She was on the edge of her bed watching the lightning of a storm explode from the same clouds that rushed the windows with a steady spray of rain. She'd told him from the doorway in his sleep. Her voice must have crossed into his dreams right alongside the coyotes and dogs down in the wash. She closed her eyes and almost fell asleep sitting and the thunder drummed her awake and she was surprised all over again to see such a powerful storm and the blocks below it where until two weeks before she had walked.

Her new roommate gasped at the strength of the storm she hadn't been able to hear from the television couch in the dayroom. Laura Pettler. Bright Laura Tuesday Pettler.

"Better monsoon than mon-later," she said and clapped and nudged her on her shoulder. She still wasn't sure how she'd ended up in her room.

Laura crossed her arms and stood at the window and her humor disappeared and she became grave and contemplative. She touched the glass with her fingertips and spoke to both Tammy and the rain, a dramatic and fake performance she couldn't stand.

"At sunrise begins the Feast of Saints Boris and Gleb to Glorious Ruthenia according to the calendar of the Holy Virgin's Byzantine Eastern Rite Catholic Church."

"Oh."

"More than oh. The history of faith and blessed salvation itself."

The storm had weakened. You could hear it spattering onto the ground from the gutters from which it spilled. She touched the dry side of the rain running down the glass. You could not break the glass. Even if you threw a chair at it you could not break the glass. Even if you fired guns at it you could not break the glass. Laura Pettler had told her so.

She turned from the window and looked down at Tammy. "My husband belongs to the Byzantine Ruthenian Eastern Rite Catholic Church. It's a glorious faith. Glorious. I was raised a Methodist but I converted once we were married."

Tammy was surprised she was married and so young. She'd figured Laura was her age, but she didn't feel like asking her for sure, since it didn't matter a pocket of two pennies.

"But," Laura said. "But he was unfaithful to me. He sings in the choir and he was unfaithful with a woman from the choir."

Even in the dark when the rain had quit running down the glass. Even in the dark she could feel the girl's face flush. She clenched her teeth and balled up her fists.

"Oh, that choir whore."

She only wore sweatshirts. You could wear them because the unit was always so cold. But now there was another reason.

"And this," she said and rolled back the sleeves and even in the dark the scars were so raw and deep and so crossed with stitches they looked like they'd given her two more minutes to live before her husband found her curled at the bottom of the shower.

She rolled down the sleeves and returned to the window and tapped her forehead and her chest and each shoulder with her fingertips. The same way the Mexican girls had when they'd brought her flowers in the hospital. She wanted one of them to be her new roommate instead.

"I didn't do it to show him. I did it to end it. How can I live without my Lord's house to look forward to every week? How can I live without the glorious gaze of icons looking straight through my heart? Icons painted by blessed monks in Ruthenia? You think, you really think I can go back with that cunt in the choir?"

Tammy wondered how she'd done it. She thought of her husband's hunting knife. Then she thought a kitchen knife. And then she decided nail file on the floor of the shower until her husband found her. In their bathroom where she put on makeup every morning.

"We have two children," she said. "But don't think I did it to get some attention. Or to get back at him. I did it because I wanted to die. I suffer so much that I want to die. Plain and simple. And I still do. But don't say a word about that in process group. Hear?"

"I won't."

"Otherwise they'll never let me out of here. I've got to get back with my kids. But how can I face them in such a house of deception?"

"How old?"

"Four and six. Girl and boy."

"They probably don't understand yet."

"But I do. I do and that's the thing!"

"I'm sorry, Laura. I'm drifting. I need to sleep."

"Oh, I never sleep anymore. I stay up all night. I stay up all night and think, think, think about everything. Everything."

They woke everyone up to line up for breakfast at seven. And then after breakfast they lined everybody up to get their meds at the nurse's window. And then everyone got their vitals.

"How many hours did you sleep?"

"Nine."

"Did you shower yesterday?"

"No."

"Do you think you're going to shower today?"

"Maybe."

"Did you move your bowels this morning?"

"No."

"Yesterday?"

"No."

"Think you might move your bowels today?"

"Yes."

And then they lined everyone up for group processing, where the patients sat at school desks in a circle and took turns checking in with the facilitator, an older lady with her hair colored red and rings of beads all down the front of her flower dress. They shared with the rest of the group for support and processing feedback. You couldn't judge and you couldn't try to fix.

"This morning I feel like we should have telephones in our rooms."

"Can't you use the telephones in the hallway?"

"Someone's always talking to their man on the telephones in the hallway. Lonnie and Sweat Pea especially."

Sweet Pea stood and pointed. She was a big Indian woman off the Pee-Posh reservation who wore eyeglasses tinted with green cigarette stains.

"Who says you own the fucking phones?"

"I didn't say I owned shit. I said you're always on them."

"You the hallway telephone police now?"

"Sit down, Sweet Pea."

"I have a right to my point of view."

"You do, Sweet Pea. But you need to sit down in order to have that point of view. Tammy, would you like to check in?"

"Pass."

You could always pass if you wanted to. Tammy had passed at every session since she'd arrived.

"Laura?"

"Yes! Today we celebrate the Glorious Feast of Saints Boris and Gleb who brought Christianity to Ruthenia according to the calendar of the Holy Virgin's Byzantine Eastern Rite Catholic Church. Wisdom. Let us be attentive. Every day gives me more reason to live."

She looked down at her palms and blinked.

"Is there anything else, Laura?"

Her face got hard and the muscles in her jaw moved.

"There is something else. I think about the way they did it. My husband and that woman from the choir. That cunt. How they did it. How they fucked."

"We're all entitled to our anger, Laura. But I'd like you to try leaving out aggressive language."

"Like cunt and fuck?"

"Yes, like cunt and fuck."

She shoved her desk and stood and slammed the door behind her. A few of the other women laughed.

"Tammy, are you sure you don't want to check in?"

"No, thank you. Pass."

"All right. How about you, Wanda?"

"What's wrong with that woman?"

"With Laura?"

"Yes."

"Let's not discuss Laura now that she's left the room."

"She's as crazy as a cat in Vaseline."

"Let's move on."

"I'm next."

"Cynthia."

"I'm in a horrible mood now after all that. Horrible. Damn bring down."

"Why do you think that had such an impact on you?"

"Aw, Cynthia, don't worry about that batshit twat."

"Charlene."

"Feast Day of Fuck. Every goddamn morning."

She felt Kayla breeze in on the air of death. On the air of her last breath from whatever room upstairs she'd died in. She felt her take the empty seat beside her that Laura had abandoned. She was naked and her body was beautiful. She whispered her check in and nobody talked over her.

"Tammy doesn't want to check in so I'll check in for her."

The room emptied and only the facilitator stayed.

"Baby Girl I hope you don't mind me checking you in."

"No."

She wondered if her own body underneath all those big clothes was as beautiful as Kayla's.

"Tammy better keep her mouth shut, or else these women are going to turn on her like a pack of bobcats. I could tell you myself but I'm protecting her. I don't have to protect her and I shouldn't. You see what they did to your friend?"

"She's not my friend."

"And neither am I."

The facilitator had left and the lights were off.

"I tried to help you, Kayla."

But Kayla had nothing more to say. Her head was gone. And then her legs and her arms and the rest of her body.

She found Laura pacing the room and biting her nails after

dinner that night. She hadn't been in the cafeteria and she hadn't seen her all day.

"For his sake I hope her pussy tastes like a sewer. Where do you think they get their dirty screwing on? I'll tell you where: they screw in the choir loft and they screw behind the iconostasis."

"You going to recreation?"

"I don't want to go any damn place but a lily casket."

In recreation they used stencils to make pictures of flowers.

"Here in recreation," the instructor said, the same way she said it every night, "we recreate. And what do we recreate?"

Tammy raised her hand. "We recreate ourselves."

"That's right. Excellent."

She thought maybe if she drew enough flowers, she'd be able to recreate herself into a whole different new person who didn't need to be drawing flowers in a place like this.

And she raised her hand the moment group processing began the next morning. Laura was back but no longer sitting beside her. She hadn't sat next to her at breakfast either.

"Tammy? I'm happy to see you want to check in."

"I'm really sad."

"What about?"

"My past. Everything in my past."

"That's a natural struggle. A universal struggle every soul on this earth pains over at times."

She held in her breath. Seconds. A wall of solid power in her chest. She let go, she said, "I've done lots of things I'm ashamed of and I can't seem to shake any of my shame."

"Do you know the difference between shame and guilt?"

"Hold on, please."

"Forgive me. Go on."

The rest of the women and their eyes bright as Laura's Tuesday and diving right out of their faces to see and to hear what she had to say next. She thought she might start crying but the tension behind her eyes slid down to the base of her spine and vanished.

"I whored. I whored myself to get drugs."

When she looked up from her desk she saw a few of the women nodding. The big Indian Sweet Pea among them.

"I did too, Tammy. I did too and so did some of us others."

There was a different bright in Laura's own face. A bright and glowing hatred. Her knuckles white on either side of her desk.

"You fuck anyone's husband?"

"Laura, that's enough."

"You suck them? Give them your head?"

"Sit the fuck down," another woman told her.

Tammy was standing too. Not to fight back, but to shield herself by running if Laura got any closer. The facilitator had opened the door and was calling for help. All the women were standing. Laura broke away from the two women holding her back. She rushed Tammy and brought her to the ground and grabbed her hair and she felt blood run out of her nose and bloom warm in her mouth like the flowers in the vase on the counter they'd brought her in the hospital and she counted with each hit one two three one two three beatings one two three beatings.

"Restraint," she heard a man call from above her. And then Laura was lifted and grunting like a handled animal as they took her away.

"Give that crazy bitch the hot Johnny," said Sweet Pea.

"She's gone, baby. Out, out, out for good."

Laura's things were gone by the time Tammy had left medical two floors up. She'd only gotten two thin cuts and a bruise on the bridge of her nose. She looked at herself in the bathroom's metal mirror. You had to get close or the reflection was nothing but blurry waves of the kind of face that pads up and down the hallways in a mental ward in blue paper slippers. But when she got close and saw, whatever hurt she'd felt quit.

They'd given her even more Thorazine and then Haldol on top of the Thorazine and on top of the lithium and there in the bathroom it all kicked in and at dinner she watched the gradual progress of her spoon move a dollop of mashed potatoes up to her mouth and felt the gradual progress of her mouth moving to chew it.

She heard one woman tell another, "He blows all his goddamn money on toys. He's got two high money guitars and three amplifiers. Dumb shit."

"What did you do?"

"I set him on fire in his bed. In my soul and in my imagination of fire."

"That would have been something seeing him on stage playing his guitar all on fire. Tammy, you married?"

"What?"

"You married?"

"No, no."

"You think you will be?"

"I used to. I used to wish I'd get married but I don't know anymore."

"You watch out you don't end up with some shit who blows all his money on musical instruments and he's not even in a band."

"You'd see him up there on stage playing the guitar all covered in flames from your fire imagination and burning to death up there for all the rock and roll crowd to see."

She was dismissed from recreation when she couldn't lift her pencil. She watched the art paper for even a little flower to grow on her behalf. In the morning there was a drawing of a flower by her feet at the end of the bed. She propped the drawing up on the windowsill and at once she wanted to get as high as Jesus Christ in the clouds. She didn't deserve this kindness.

She wasn't sure how this kind of news made it to the unit, but the worst news about those who'd recently left always did. Laura had broken her bathroom mirror. She'd only been home two days. She'd broken her bathroom mirror and took a long shard into the shower and her children had found her.

"Now they're dead," Tammy said to the other women in the dayroom, none of whom would sit on the couch.

"No, only Laura's dead."

She shrugged and ambled to the nurse's station.

"What do I have to do to get out of here?"

"The attending psychiatrist has to approve your discharge."

"How do I sign myself out?"

"Even if you AMA, Doctor Wood still needs to approve it."

"What's an AMA?"

"Against medical advice."

Doctor Wood only asked her one question: "Do you have any plans of harming yourself?"

And when she said no, he told her she could go.

She almost went back when she remembered she'd left the drawing by the window. She turned and looked at the door, then up at what she imagined had been her window to see if the drawing was trying to jump. Not to her, but to jump. She tried to walk normally but her feet couldn't seem to lift into a full and confident step. She stopped and almost walked back when she remembered she hadn't said goodbye. But by then she'd turned too many corners and the hospital was nowhere behind her.

She passed the apartment complex where Tomahawk Junior had lived. Later, Stylish Price's complex. And later, Santiago's house. She stopped before each of them but didn't go to any of the doors. The heat was a tree of orange coils fallen around her. And once she kept walking, Santiago called to her.

"We heard you were dead."

"No."

"Good, man. Good. Come on. Come in and celebrate life."

They were sprawled all over the couch and on the floor and in the beanbag. The room was candles and black spoons and spikes. She recognized some of them, but nobody knew her. Then one of the men asked where she'd been.

"I went back to Oklahoma."

"Oklahoma rock and rolla."

"What happened to your face?"

"My mom kicked my ass."

"What the fuck for?"

"Listening to metal."

"What metal?"

"Dokken."

"Rockin' Dokken."

"She said it was Satan's music."

"Isn't it?"

"She tried to make me eat the tape."

"How the fuck you eat a tape?"

"You open wide."

Santiago had fixed another spike so she might celebrate life. She felt the hospital drugs wiggle out of her bloodstream to make room for it.

"Shoot it, jack it," somebody said.

She was pretty sure the Greyhound station was only a block or so away.

"Where she going?"

"Where you going?"

"She thinks Satan's music is in that hype, man. Santiago, if she doesn't want it."

"I want to make a collect call to Susan Judson."

"Will you accept a collect call from Tammy Holt?"

"Like hell I'll accept it."

"Look, I want to make a collect call to Susan Judson."

"I have a collect call from Tammy Holt. Will you accept the charges?"

"Shit. Fine."

"I'm not high, Mama."

"How do I know that?"

"You just have to believe me. Or you can hang up."

"Last time I believed you, you sucked all my money right up your nose."

"You've got every right to hang up on me."

"Don't think I don't know that for a second, Tammy. Where's your father?"

"California, I guess."

"Where are you?"

"I'm in Phoenix, Arizona. I love you, Mama. And you've got every right to hang up on me. Every right in the world."

The deputies led the trustees off the bus at dawn and the chains locked around their ankles clanged down the steps and their boots scraped the gravel once they reached the ground. The deputies carried shotguns and the men wore faded stripes with *MCSO* printed across their backs.

The caskets arrived in the back of a pickup truck. Pine boxes that had been made in the woodshop at the state prison in Perryville. One of the caskets no bigger than a cooler. Preacher Meet carried it himself and the trustees and the deputies followed him into the part of the cemetery they called Baby Land. Two men lowered it into the grave with lengths of twine and one of the others said, "I don't deserve to be remembered either," and he stepped back and covered his mouth and then his eyes and two trustees took him under his arms when they saw his knees go. The deputies looked away over the rest of the desert and the rows of anonymous plots it held.

The men held their hands over the casket and lowered their heads and Preacher Meet paused in his prayers whenever a low-flying jet roared across the sky above them.

"Amen," he said.

"Amen."

The men put their arms down and watched the little casket and Preacher Meet asked them if they wanted to name the infant.

"Angel," one of them said. "Because that's where she is now. An angel who walks with the Lord."

In whispers the trustees counted on three and lifted the last casket over the truck hatch with half a foot of space between them and carried it to the hole just on the other side of Baby Land. They were drenched and under the sweat filthy with the cemetery dirt that had already turned into a film of mud on their arms and hands. The sun burned with more fury every inch it rose and between burials the deputies led them to the tank on the back of the bus for water that had about an hour left of cold to it. They could taste it leaving every time they took a drink.

A fire breath blew a pair of tumbleweeds across the markers and across the road and across more dead land until they got wedged in a stand of brittlebush and stilled as though defeated by their capture.

"They're all babies when they enter the Kingdom of Heaven. All babies. Gentle and tender and without sin. We hurt more than they do. We cry but they smile. We cry but they smile forever."

Another wind and the tumbleweeds came loose off the brittle-bush and bounced away rolling across the desert the deputies watched through their sunglasses.

"This man's name is Weldon Holt. Most of the dead here have no names. Yet Weldon Holt still knew who he was, and he must have remembered the names of those who'd forgotten him."

The trustees lowered his casket into the ground with straps. Three men on one side and three men on the other. Lot 12, Row 2, Space 7. A marker no bigger than a bar of soap. Charitable visitors would glance down at it on their way to bring flowers to Baby Land.

7

Her mother got her a job at the high school cafeteria preparing and serving potatoes and green beans and gravy for their ham and chicken fried steak. At the same time she had to make sure none of them grabbed more than one cup of pudding. This was the best part of the job. She didn't like looking at any of their faces as they slid their trays past her. She'd grown twenty pounds heavier than when they'd last seen her, but by their whispers she knew they still knew who she was.

Her mother had been promoted to cafeteria manager and after the students had finished, they would eat in the kitchen with the other two cafeteria women who only spoke to one another at the table on the other side of the room. They'd spoken to Tammy only once when she'd first started, and coldly. Hello. And not another word since.

"They got GED classes up at the Rawlins Community Center," her mother told her.

"Oh."

And then they cleaned the serving trays and wiped down the tables and counters and drink machines. Tammy took the trash out, two big black plastic bags stuffed with wrappers and plastic and the dripping sludge of food waste. She smoked even though her break had just ended half an hour before. She watched the flat cold metal sky that didn't move either east or west. It sat watching her, a lid pressed over today and tomorrow and the next week and on into her forever. She was halfway down her cigarette when Peggy Alkire came out with a look in her face as bleak as the sky.

"You already had your break," she told her. "County don't pay you to smoke cigarettes and watch the clouds float on by."

The woman crossed her arms and made sure she stomped it out. "Well don't leave it there," she said. "Put it in the dumpster. Otherwise it's just more work for me to sweep up later."

She tossed it in the garbage and put her head down and stuck her hands in her pockets and headed back to the door and the woman told her shoulders, "I got a daughter your age who wouldn't mind a job like yours. She wouldn't mind getting the job you got. It's good having a cafeteria supervisor for a mama, isn't it? It's a good way to get your foot in the door."

She handed her paycheck over to her mother every other Friday and she was never allowed to have the station wagon. She was surprised her mother let her leave the house at all. But the little house was all the way out on County Road H and the wind was already biting and town was an hour away by foot. Her mother rented the house from a beet farmer and Tammy would at dusk and on Sunday afternoons walk the farmer's field, the dirt still rows of clumps where the sugar beets had been harvested and sent to the sugar beet plant that pushed its rolling clouds of smoke into the sky to form a high heaven of stink.

The slices of white ice on either side of the cold brook were growing across the water. It ran on the edge of the field furthest from the house under the bare branches the long trees that divided the property from County Road H, where the trucks ran packed with beets and beet sugar and across the road the railroad tracks where freights rumbled past loaded with car after car of coal from Gillette, Wyoming and the depth of her shame ran the length of the brook and the road and the length of the train and all the tracks it ran on.

She tried to make it back to the house in one walk. She felt the shame rise into her face. Into her eyes especially. They would see everything she'd done. She sat down in the middle of the field with her legs crossed and watched the end of the day. Nothing moved. Not even the sky. No brook, no trucks, no train. She opened her coat and put her hand over her heart.

Her mother made her empty her pockets when she got home. She even dug around the bottom of her Marlboro box.

"You put your butts in the creek?"

"No," she said, and produced the nubs of wrinkled filters from her coat pocket.

"Five? You've only been gone a little over an hour."

"I get nervous."

"Nervous about what? There's nothing out there but dirt."

Her younger sister Janey had been living with her father, but she visited on weekends and seemed to have grown a whole decade in the year Tammy had been gone. Her voice had deepened with an edge that drove a quiet scrutiny through the few questions she asked.

"You think you'll get a new boyfriend now that you're home?"

"I'm not sure about that. Not for a while at least."

And, "What's it like to live on the street?"

"I never lived on the street."

"Mama said you did."

"Janey," her mother said. "That's about enough."

On Monday she decided not to smoke when she took the kitchen garbage out. But Peggy Alkire had watched her go out with the bags and came out to catch her anyway.

"Were you going to smoke?"

"No."

"I got a daughter your age."

"I know."

"She wouldn't mind getting a job like yours."

The next day Peggy Alkire called in sick and Tammy took a

number of breaks her mother was too busy to notice. And after lunch when she tucked herself up against the side of the dumpster, Peggy Alkire's daughter Dorothy came around the corner of the building and flinched when she saw Tammy.

"Shit," Dorothy said. "Sorry," she said, then looked at the ground and turned away.

"No, it's fine," Tammy told her.

"You graduated last year, right?"

"No, I was out in California with my dad."

"California?"

"California."

"That must have been nice."

"It was warm. Sunny."

"Not like this. Makes me so goddamn depressed."

"Me too."

"You go to the beach?"

"We went to the beach every weekend."

"Wow. Weren't you afraid of sharks out in the water?"

"I just mostly laid out in the sand."

"I can tell. You still look tan."

"Tammy?"

"Shit," she said. Her mother was calling for her out the back door. "See you around," she said over her shoulder.

"Okay," Dorothy told her.

"Was that Dorothy Alkire?"

"Yes."

"What does she want? She should be home looking after her mother. You know she had a baby last year."

"Boy or girl?"

"That isn't the point. Here," she said, tapping the counter by the sink. "Empty out your pockets."

There was snow. It covered the field with a white silence and even the trains and the trucks lost all their sounds when she watched them pass. The brook was frozen over, but she could still see a little water running underneath the ice. In the middle of the field she was a perfect spot from the sky. And then the second snow came she walked the word HELP with her boots to see if anyone circling up there might land to see what was wrong. She would get in with him as long as she didn't have to do anything and as long as he promised to fly her up to some mountains.

She served them ham and she served them potatoes and peas and corn and Peggy Alkire said, "Slow it down. You're bunching up my line." In front of them all, and they watched her to see how she'd react. She kept it all down in her gut, but they could tell, all of them, and they watched. And when they were gone, Peggy Alkire watched her while she wiped down the tables, waiting for a defensive confrontation. But Tammy had lost all her strength for conflict. She felt her shoulders tighten and craved a drink and a line as long as the way back to Phoenix, Arizona. She could make herself pop like a palm tree in flames.

Dorothy was out by the dumpster when she took out the trash. She was smoking and she offered Tammy one.

"I can't stay out here too long," Tammy said. "Your mom is going to get pissed."

"Don't listen to her bullshit. She's pissed at the whole goddamn world because she hasn't had any dick in twenty years. Watch."

She banged on the back door and yelled, "Peggy! Peggy Alkire there's a big old chocolate cake out here for you."

And when Peggy came to the door and saw her daughter standing there and laughing, she said, "Why aren't you in class, girl?"

"They told me I was smart enough to leave when I wanted to."

"I'm fixing to slap you across the mouth."

"That right? You fixing to slap me?"

"Look at that," Dorothy said, once her mother went back inside. "Talk, talk, talk and no shit to shake."

For the first time she noticed that Dorothy's eyes were red and heavy. She was stoned.

"Here," Dorothy said. "A little present for having to serve biscuits and puke to people you can't stand. Here," she said, and stuck a joint in Tammy's hand.

"I appreciate it. But I don't know."

"What, you find Jesus out in California."

"No."

"Then puff the gray skies away."

"All right."

"I have to pick up my baby off my grandma. Let me know how that goes down."

Most of the snow in the field had melted and she laid back on the crunch of the frozen slush after she smoked the whole joint. It felt good until she spotted some stars through the clouds and remembered all the ways she used to keep track of the stained days and when she tried to sit up the coat held her down like a man had crawled into it and then she was trying to run back to the house and tripping over the clumps of dirt and the ice and she imagined what her father's voice would sound like calling her name from behind her through the screech of the train and the trucks and the gush of the brook if it ever flooded and busted the ice and turned into a river he'd never be able to cross.

"I want to call my daddy," she told her mother. She'd started crying to hide the weed red in her eyes but now a real sorrow had taken hold. She'd hurried to the phone in the kitchen and waited, wiping her eyes, for her mother to give her the number. "I want to talk to him. I want to tell him I'm sorry."

"Tammy."

"Give me his number."

"I tried to call but his number was disconnected."

"He would have called for me."

"I know it. I know he would have."

"Give me his number."

"He's not there. It's disconnected."

"If he's missing you should call the police."

"I did."

"When? When did you call the police?"

"Honey, I just found out last week. I talked to the county."

"Where is he? Where is he, Mama?"

"He died. He died five months ago. He died in Phoenix. He was drunk on the street. I'm sorry, honey. I was still trying to figure out how to tell you."

She stayed home sick the next morning and urged herself back to sleep every time she awoke to find the green spots on the ceiling that were plastic stars that lit up glowing whenever you shut off the lights. They'd been up there since she was a girl. She got up once and stood on the bed to peel them off. But she knew her mother loved her and didn't want to hurt her feelings. She wasn't startled when somebody knocked on her bedroom window because she already knew it was Dorothy with her baby girl Rose.

"I let you in the front," she said through the glass.

"My mom told me you were sick."

They sat on the front room floor and let the baby grab at her feet and rock and babble. Dorothy's eyes were clean this time.

"I've been down all day in bed," Tammy said.

"Fever?"

"Bad fever. I shouldn't even be this close to your baby."

Dorothy felt Tammy's forehead with the back of her hand. "Feels like it broke," she said. "Besides, she's a little boulder. She doesn't seem to catch anything. But I better let you get back to resting."

"Wait, don't go yet. I'm not really sick."

"What's wrong?"

"I found out last night that my daddy died."

"Tammy."

"He was homeless in Phoenix. Drunk."

Baby Rose had fallen asleep. They sat on the front stoop and smoked in the cold. A wind came off the field that smelled like the wet earth it blew across. Sometimes the sun shone, but most of the day the thick sky walled itself over the rays.

"I think I walked right past him once. On the street. I didn't want to recognize him until now. But I'm pretty sure that was him. I thought he was just a bum. Guess he was."

"What happened to you out there?"

They'd left the door open a crack and they heard the baby wake up crying and Dorothy went in and picked her up and patted her and told Tammy she was really sorry about her dad.

"I don't know what to say, Tammy. I'm afraid I'll say the wrong thing."

Janey had moved back in a week before and when she got home from school that day she went into Tammy's room and stood by her bed. "I'm really sorry about your daddy."

"Thank you."

"What did he die of?"

"He got real sick."

"Sick with what?"

"He got sick drinking too much liquor."

She patted the side of the bed and motioned for Janey to sit.

"I didn't know you could die from that."

"You can if you drink enough."

"Was he nice?"

"Guess he wasn't so nice when I was a baby, which is why Mama took me and moved all the way back up here."

"From California?"

"From California."

"Did he always drink too much?"

"No. He quit for a really long time."

"Was he nice when he quit?"

"Very nice."

"Did you love him?"

"I did."

"He loved you too."

"I know it."

"What did he do?"

"For work?"

"Yes."

"He drove trucks for a long time. All over the country. But he got hurt in his back and he had to go on disability."

"Did you drink a lot of liquor when you were gone?"

"I don't think you should know about that yet, Janey."

"I guess that means you did."

"I guess it does."

She never went back to her job at the school cafeteria and her mother hired Dorothy Alkire to replace her. She wouldn't let Dorothy pay her for watching Rose every day.

"Don't you think you can use that money?" her mother asked her.

"It's only until summer."

"Summer's quite a while away."

She showed baby Rose the field and carried her up and down its rows and sat with her on the edge of the brook that ran clear now that the ice had melted and she showed her the trucks and she showed her the trains that would sometimes lull her to sleep. She felt alone and not alone, this life resting her head on her shoulder, so still she didn't want to disturb her by walking back to the house, and she wouldn't be able to walk here at all.

She forgot what her father's voice had sounded like, a burial inside her that vanished without a headstone to visit. She wondered if her mother remembered it, but she was terrified of finding out that it was within her and within her alone that the last of his voice had died. She listened hard to try to bring it back, her eyes pinched shut, but she could only see his mouth, the way it had told her hello and the way it had worried and the way it had tried to save her and soon even that was gone.

ACKNOWLEDGMENTS

Thank you: Eric Miles Williamson, Ron Cooper, Jonathan Lyons, William Hastings, Adrian Van Young, Janique Jouin, Aurelien Masson, Yoko Lacour, Joseph D. Haske, and Daniel M. Mendoza.

PATRICK MICHAEL FINN is the author of the novella *A Martyr for Suzy Kosasovich* and the story collection *From the Darkness Right Under Our Feet*. He lives in Mesa, Arizona with his wife, poet Valerie Bandura, and their son.

On the following pages are a few
more great titles from the
Down & Out Books publishing family.

For a complete list of books and to
sign up for our newsletter,
go to DownAndOutBooks.com.

Radicals
Nik Korpon

Down & Out Books
May 2021
978-1-64396-185-9

When a mysterious cyber-terrorist organization begins erasing Americans' medical debt, enigmatic FBI cybercrimes agent Jay Brodsky must focus on an attack threatening to destabilize the US economy.

But when the trail leads to his own family, Jay will be forced to confront everything he never knew about his parents and his long-missing sister and decide where his true loyalties lie.

She Talks to Angels
A Henry Malone Novel
James D.F. Hannah

Down & Out Books
May 2021
978-1-64396-173-6

2019 Shamus Award Nominee for Best Paperback Original!

Meadow Charles had plenty of secrets to hide—and someone left her dead in a land fill to keep those secrets hidden. The man who confessed to the crime now says he's innocent, and he needs Henry Malone to prove it.

Henry will have to explore one family's dark past—and confront someone willing to murder to keep those secrets buried!

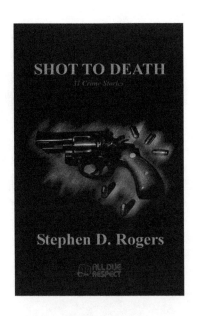

Shot to Death
31 Crime Stories
Stephen D. Rogers

All Due Respect, an imprint of
Down & Out Books
April 2021
978-1-64396-193-4

Thirty-one bullets that will leave you gasping for breath…

From hardboiled to noir to just plain human, these stories allow you to experience lives you escaped, and to do so with dignity, humor, and an eye toward tomorrow.

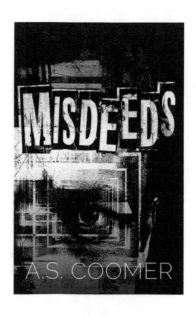

Misdeeds
A Criminal Collection of Crime Fiction
A.S. Coomer

Shotgun Honey, an imprint of
Down & Out Books
May 2021
978-1-64396-110-1

This is a book of *Misdeeds*. The stories between these covers will shock, appall, and enthrall.

There are killers in here. Thieves & vagabonds, needy sisters & disgruntled brothers, cops & kidnapers, not to mention a corruptor of children, all slide around the pages of *Misdeeds* like burning grease in an overheated pan.

These stories pop, sizzle, and burn. Consider yourself warned, fresh meat.

CPSIA information can be obtained
at www.ICGtesting.com
Printed in the USA
FSHW010747060621
82135FS